# The Scent of Blood

# Raymond Miller

# The Scent of Blood

A Nathaniel Singer P.I. Novel

*The* Toby Press

*The Scent of Blood*
*The* Toby Press LLC
First edition 2006

POB 8531, New Milford, CT. 06776-8531, USA
*&* POB 2455, London WIA 5WY, England
www.tobypress.com

© Raymond Miller

ISBN-10 1 59264 184 9, ISBN-13 978 1 59264 184 0, *paperback*

A CIP catalogue record for this title is
available from the British Library

Printed and bound in the United States
by Thomson-Shore Inc., Michigan

JUL 10 2007

*163188*

MYSTERY

# Chapter one

She was a woman who had once been beautiful and would someday be beautiful again. That much was obvious. Even now, when she looked as if she hadn't slept in weeks, and her face was swollen from weeping, she was one of the most striking women I'd ever seen.

But observations like this were merely personal. She had come to me for professional help.

"I'm sorry," she said. "I thought I was going to be able to control myself. But I can't talk about it or think about it without feeling like I'm going to fall apart."

There was a box of tissues on my desk. I pushed it toward her.

Sometimes I feel like I'm a psychiatrist. Sometimes I wish I *were* a psychiatrist. The pay would be better and I wouldn't get beaten up as much. But for better or for worse, I'm a private detective.

"There's no hurry, Mrs. Carpenter. Take as much time as you need."

She put a tissue to her nose and blew, with a loud honking noise that didn't match the rest of her. Her features were delicate and her skin was pale and flawless. She had the air of a figure from a Renaissance painting.

"My husband was killed by a hit-and-run driver, three weeks ago. The police say there's no reason to believe it was anything other than an accident. But I know it wasn't an accident. I know it."

"How do you know it, Mrs. Carpenter?"

"Would death threats count as a good reason?"

"Your husband received death threats?"

"He'd been getting death threats for the past three months."

"Do you know who the death threats were coming from?"

"The notes were signed by the 'Party of God.'"

I'd never heard of them.

"What's the Party of God?"

"It's what it sounds like. It's a group of religious fanatics."

"Why were they threatening him?"

"My husband was a doctor. He was a brilliant doctor, and he was also a brilliant researcher. He was doing research with embryonic stem cells and was lucky enough to get some publicity for his efforts—last summer there was a cover story in the *New York Times Magazine*. And that's when the death threats started. They told him he was a baby-killer. They said if he didn't stop his research..."

She didn't finish the sentence, and didn't need to.

"Where did your husband practice?"

"At Sloan-Kettering."

"What was his specialty?"

"He was a pediatric heart surgeon. He was the head of pediatric surgery."

She looked proud as she said this, and, although I try not to think about my own personal life when I'm working, I briefly wondered what it must be like to be married to a woman who is proud of you.

"I can understand why you want someone to look into this, Mrs. Carpenter. I'm wondering why you decided to ask me."

I'm good at what I do, but I've never been high-profile, and if I had to guess I would have guessed that Mrs. Carpenter dealt only with the most high-profile vendors, no matter what services she was seeking. New York is filled with boutique detective agencies; establishments with gleaming conference rooms and busy research departments and framed letters of thanks from captains of industry and foreign dignitaries and movie stars, alluding mysteriously to indispensable services rendered. All I had was my two-room office with a Mr. Coffee in the corner and a part-time secretary who at the moment was nowhere to be seen.

"I got your number from Susannah Parker," she said. "She said you're good. And she said I could trust you."

Susannah Parker was a client I'd had almost ten years earlier. "I'm glad she remembers me."

"Will you help me, Mr. Singer?"

"Mrs. Carpenter, I can try. But you need to understand from the beginning that the chances I'll find anything out are very slim. I'll interview the witnesses, I'll find out what I can about the Party of God. But you should understand that we're unlikely to discover anything. The cops are pretty thorough when they investigate a hit-and-run, so I don't know if I'm going to learn anything they haven't already told you."

Mrs. Carpenter looked disappointed, and I thought she was going to get up and leave.

When someone asks me to work on a case that seems hopeless, I always give them a speech like this. I don't want them to end up feeling like I've stolen their money. I want them to know the odds. About fifty percent of the time, the prospective client finds my speech so discouraging that he or she thanks me for my time, leaves my office, and never gets in touch with me again. I've lost thousands of dollars along the line, but it's helped me keep a clear conscience.

"If Susannah hadn't told me about you," she said, "I think I'd leave right now and look for someone willing to assure me that he could help. But she said one of the things that she valued about you was that you never made promises you couldn't keep. Susannah warned me that you'd tell me that there probably wasn't much you'd be able to do. But she also said that she'd never met anyone who was more persistent than you are. She said that if the truth is out there to be found, you'd find it."

I told her my fee. As she reached into her purse and hunted around for her checkbook, I was able to study her.

There are people who can make you believe in an aristocracy of nature. People so attractive, so elegant, so assured, that they seem to belong to some other realm. Natalie Carpenter was one of those people. She was tall, and slim, and her eyes were a dark shade of sea-green that I'd never seen before. She was the kind of person who probably seemed in command of just about every situation that came her way. If I'd met her anyplace else, the thought that she might need my help would have been unimaginable. But the street where I plied my trade was not quite like anyplace else.

# Chapter two

I couldn't get to her case that day, or the next. I had some other work I needed to do. When I did turn to Mrs. Carpenter's case, the first thing I did was call a cop I knew, a guy named Keller, who worked in homicide

"Morning, Singer," he said, before I'd even said hello. Only ten or fifteen years behind the general public, the NYPD had finally installed Caller ID on its telephones. "Read any good books lately?"

He had once seen a couple of books in my car, and five years later, the memory still seemed to amuse him.

Keller was a decent guy, and we got along, but we'd never been the best of friends. Like most cops, he disliked freelancers. During my first few years as a detective, cops would go out of their way *not* to help me. But I'd stuck around, and done my job, and most of them tolerated me now; some of them, like Keller, actually owed me. I had once helped his son out of a jam, a situation that nobody else in Keller's universe would have been able to deal with. So after that, when I needed him, he helped me out.

"I got a visit from Natalie Carpenter the other day," I said. "You ever heard of her?"

"The doctor's widow, right? Yeah, she came around here a couple of times after her husband died, telling us how to do our job. She still thinks it wasn't an accident?"

"That's what she thinks. Is she wrong?"

"Of course she's wrong. He walked out into the middle of traffic without looking and somebody ran him down."

"Nobody got a license plate?"

"Nope."

"You looked into the death threats?"

"Death threats?"

"Letters. From some outfit called the Party of God."

Mrs. Carpenter had had the death threats delivered to my office. They were closely argued, semi-literate, and filled with exclamation points.

"First I heard about them. I wasn't following closely. It wasn't my case."

"Could you do me a favor, Keller?"

"Somehow I knew that was coming."

"I promised her I'd find out what I could. I told her I was sure you people had done everything right, and that if the cops said it was just a hit-and-run, then it was just a hit-and-run. But I'd like to be able to be sure about it. I'd like to be able to tell her that you guys looked into the death threats and had a good reason to tell her that the Party of God had nothing to do with his death."

"Well, I guess I can take a few minutes and ask around about it. Women like her can be a pain in the ass."

I knew what he was thinking. Photogenic, well-connected, intelligent, bereaved, and convinced that the police screwed up—a woman like Mrs. Carpenter tends to get the attention of the media. So it was in Keller's interest to find a way to reassure Mrs. Carpenter that New York's Finest had done all they could.

The other part of it, though, the part that Keller would never own up to, was that even if women like Mrs. Carpenter weren't a pain in the ass, he probably would have helped me anyway. He was basically a good guy, and if he could do me a favor without inconveniencing himself too much, he would do it.

He called me back about an hour later.

"Turns out that we did look into the death threats, but it went nowhere. There was nothing there."

"What makes you say that?"

"It just smelled wrong. When one of these nut job organizations kill somebody, they never make it look like an accident. They don't call us up and say they did it, but they never make it look like an accident. They want people to know."

"That makes sense."

"I'm glad you approve. Of course it makes sense. They want everybody to know, because the point is never to take out one particular doctor, the point is always to scare off as many doctors as they can. The guy I talked to said the consensus was that she wrote those letters herself."

"Why would she do that?"

"Why would she do that? That's not the kind of question I can answer. I'm still a beat cop at heart. You're the brainy independent. You're the one with the insight into the human soul."

After we got off the phone, I answered a few emails, and then I turned my computer on and googled "Party of God." I got more than ninety thousand hits. Evidently there were two Parties of God, which had nothing to do with each other: an Islamic terrorist organization based in Lebanon, and a born-again Christian organization based in Rockland County, New York. The group in Rockland County, among its many concerns, believed that God was being mocked by those who performed medical research with embryonic stem cells. The Islamic organization, preoccupied as it was with stopping the Zionist infidel from taking over the world, didn't seem to care much about embryonic stem cells. This was fortunate for me, since Rockland County was less than two hours away from the city. It would have been a drag to have to go all the way to Lebanon to investigate this thing.

## Chapter three

The Party of God's headquarters were about two hours north of the city. The organization was housed in a gleaming but nondescript modern building, set off by itself in an estate of about five acres. It had its own parking lot, the entrance booth of which was manned by a muscular gentleman whose small, dark, boxy moustache made him look as if his great regret in life was that he had been born too late to join the Nazi Party in its glory days. He looked not so much like Hitler, as Charlie Chaplin playing Hitler in *The Great Dictator.*

"May I help you?" he said, with an expression that seemed to say that strangling me would actually be his preference.

"I'm here to see Dr. Frye." The acting director of the organization.

"Do you have an appointment?"

"Yes. I do."

By "I," I was not quite referring to myself as I actually was, but to the "I" who had spoken to Frye's secretary earlier that day. I'd told her I was a freelance journalist working on an article about religion in America today. I had a tight deadline, and Dr. Frye had been able to squeeze me in.

The poet Rimbaud once famously declared that "I is someone else." This would be a handy slogan for a private detective, who has to be someone else every couple of weeks or so in the line of duty.

"One moment." He picked up the receiver of his phone. After a minute he put down the receiver and waved me past.

He looked disappointed to be letting me in. Somehow he had already sized me up as a pro-choice, anti-prayer-in-the-public-schools, free-speech-loving Jew. Sized me up correctly, I might add.

I was met at the front door by a small, very demurely dressed young woman.

"Mr. Singer?"

"Yes."

"I'm Dr. Frye's secretary. Amy Roth. We spoke this morning."

I put out my hand and she somehow accomplished the feat of shaking it while cowering away from me at the same time. Either she too had had word that I was part of the Jewish free-thinking conspiracy, or else she was very shy.

"Walk this way, please," she said, and led me down the hall to her office.

"Dr. Frye is on a conference call. He asked me to apologize and to make sure you feel at home. Would you like any coffee or tea?"

"No. Thank you."

"Is there anything I can get you? We have some literature here, if you'd like to learn more about our organization and its mission."

She handed me several brochures. I leafed through them as I waited. They confirmed the impression I'd gotten when I'd looked at the Party of God's website the night before.

The Party of God seemed to have a split personality. Some of the articles on its website appeared to have been written by men who were foaming at the mouth, deranged by hate. But some of them—chiefly the ones that had been posted in the last six months or so—were much smoother, much more polished. It wasn't as if the politics of the organization had changed. They still seemed to long for an America cleansed of everyone but the racially pure. They had just found a more acceptable way of expressing themselves.

The Party of God's founder had died a year earlier, and after a few months of uncertainty, Dr. Frye had succeeded him. I assumed Frye was responsible for the organization's new, more human, tone.

Normally, of course, while waiting in a secretary's office one would be checking out the secretary in addition to whatever else one was doing, but Amy Roth was so self-effacing as to be invisible. She sat at her desk, typing away at her computer, and she had artfully arranged the monitor so that anyone sitting on the waiting room couch would have difficulty seeing her face. If she were a cartoon character, a character with a super power, her power would have been the ability to make you forget she was in the room.

"Mr. Singer?" A tall and elegantly dressed man was standing at the threshold of an adjoining office. "Arthur Frye," he said. "Delighted to meet you." He had a good strong handshake—if, that is, it is philosophically possible to characterize anything about a right-wing hate-monger as "good."

Now that Frye had entered the room, his secretary was no longer in hiding. "You have six messages," she said, and handed him a fistful of memos. You could see awe and sheer love in her eyes.

He ushered me into his office and closed the door. As soon as I said yes to his offer of a drink, Amy Roth slipped into the room carrying a tray with coffee and tea. After Frye and I had served ourselves and sat down, she disappeared as noiselessly as she had come.

"Now tell me how I can be of assistance, Mr. Singer. My secretary was a little unsure when I asked her what you're writing about. Are you writing something general about religion in America today, or are you focusing specifically on the Party of God?"

"Actually, what I'm writing about is even more specific than that. I'm writing an article about the death of Dr. Andrew Carpenter."

Frye lifted his eyebrows in a vague, puzzled way. "I don't believe I know that name."

"Andrew Carpenter was a doctor in Manhattan, a pediatric heart surgeon. He was also a researcher. Some of his most promising work in the last two years involved using embryonic stem cells to repair heart damage in infants. There was an article about him in the *Times* a few months back, and shortly after that he began receiving death threats. Signed by the Party of God. Earlier this month he was struck and killed by a hit-and-run driver outside his workplace—less than a block from the place where he was carrying on 'the Godless labors that will bring a very speedy death and an eternity of the agony of hellfire,' as one of the letters put it."

Dr. Frye was oddly unruffled. He didn't seem to be particularly bothered that I was accusing his organization of murder. "First, Mr. Singer, I assure you that I've never heard of this man. If he was engaged in the work you describe, then the Party of God does indeed believe that he is now enduring a punishment that will last through Judgment Day and beyond. I can only rejoice that he's no longer pursuing his work. To employ a human embryo, an entity with a soul, an entity that is fully human in the eyes of God, as a guinea-pig for medical research, is an abomination. It's murder, plain and simple, and I rejoice that this murderer has been prevented from continuing his heinous work. About the death threats, however, you're quite mistaken. The Party of God is an educational organization. We engage in advocacy, but purely by means of reason and moral suasion. We do not advocate violence, and we would never issue a death threat against anyone, no matter how strongly we disagree with his views or his actions. We take Paul's epistle to the Romans very seriously."

"I can't recall that epistle," I said. "Offhand."

"'Vengeance is mine, sayeth the Lord.' Vengeance is God's prerogative. It would be blasphemous to do the work that the Lord has exclusively claimed as his own domain."

I didn't bother to argue with him about the medical use of embryonic stem cells. I could have pointed out that millions of embryos are discarded by fertility clinics every year, and that instead of ending up in Dumpsters they could be used to help find cures to diseases from diabetes to Parkinson's to Alzheimer's, but he had already heard all this, and I'd already heard everything he might say in response. I reached into the inner pocket of my jacket, brought out copies of two of the death threats and pushed them across the desk.

He took out of a pair of eyeglasses, looked at the notes, and shook his head. "Not us."

"I realize that it's not an official statement. It's not on your letterhead. But doesn't this seem like the general point of view of your group?"

"I told you, Mr. Singer. We're purely an advocacy organization. We don't believe in achieving our goals by force."

"Your organization doesn't have a more muscular arm?"

"The only force we use is the force of faith."

He stood up and extended his arm.

"I fit you into my schedule today because you told my secretary that you were on a deadline. But I have other responsibilities I must attend to now."

I shook his hand. "Thank you, Dr. Frye."

"My pleasure, Mr. Singer. I hope you'll pick up some of our complimentary literature on the way out."

He accompanied me into the outer office and began to talk to his secretary. Then the door was opened by a large man, and things began to get interesting.

"Hello, Arthur," the man said. "Entertaining members of the media again, I hear?"

Frye introduced us: "Jonathan, this is Nathaniel Singer. He's a freelance journalist. I've just helped him clear up some of his mistaken impressions about our mission. Mr. Singer, this is the Reverend Jonathan Underwood. The Reverend Underwood is the Party of God's Secretary Treasurer."

When we shook hands, my hand vanished from sight. I'm big enough, but Underwood was huge—not so far from seven feet tall.

"You're a writer?" Underwood said.

"Yes, sir."

"Is that how your knuckles got like that? Hitting the typewriter too hard?"

I have thick scarred knuckles from hitting people on the chin too hard.

"I used to be in the Golden Gloves," I said.

"Sure." He looked at me steadily. I didn't look away.

I sensed a hint of frustration as he sized me up. It was obvious that he was used to intimidating people, merely with his size. I wasn't intimidated, and he must have known it.

"Dr. Frye likes reporters," he said. "I hate them."

"I'm sorry to hear that."

"Whenever I see a reporter, I have this itch to pick them up and toss them out the window."

"Spoken like a true man of God," I said.

Underwood was glaring at me from his great height, but he seemed to be at a loss about what to say next. Coming across someone whom he wasn't able to dominate through his sheer bulk must have been an unfamiliar experience for him.

Frye was still in the doorway of his office, and Amy was at her desk. Frye looked as if he was pretending that he wasn't in the room. A conflict avoider, is what I might have called him if I were a shrink. He didn't approve of Underwood, but he wasn't about to put him in his place either. Which I found strange, since Frye was supposedly running the show.

Amy's reaction was even more notable. She stared at me, then at Underwood, then at me, as if he and I were in a tennis match. I don't know what was so shocking to her, but she looked shocked.

"Hope to see you again real soon," Underwood said. "Maybe sooner than you think."

He pushed past me into Frye's office, sat in the chair I'd just vacated, and put his feet up on Frye's desk. I'd never seen the second-in-command of an organization put his feet on the boss's desk.

# Chapter four

By the time I got out of there it was about five o'clock. It was just getting dark.

As I drove back to the city I tried to sort out what I'd learned. I'd learned that Frye was a smooth customer, too polished and too smart to be sending out death threats. But I'd also learned that his second-in-command was a loose cannon. It didn't take much imagination to see Underwood plowing somebody down with a car.

Driving through Nyack I passed an interesting-looking toy store and parked the car to check it out. Jack's birthday was coming up and I didn't want to miss it again.

The toy store turned out to be a bust. It was one of those politically correct toy stores: it didn't carry soldiers; it didn't carry toy guns; it didn't carry battery-powered trucks; it didn't carry anything my son was likely to be interested in. When I've looked for presents for my daughter Wini, I've once or twice made the mistake of asking for Barbies in places like this, and inevitably I've been met by withering looks. In my profession, I've come across some very bad men, who've given me some very hard looks, but none of them has ever given me a look more withering than the looks I've gotten from the employees of toney toy stores after I've asked whether they carry Barbie dolls. People who work in toy stores can be the scariest mugs of all.

I got back in the car. Since I was in no hurry and the surroundings were pleasant, I decided to take the local streets back to the city.

I was on a hilly road just south of Piermont when I saw a black Hummer—a vehicle designed to look like a combination of a tank and a rhinoceros—way back in the rear view mirror. It was still there five minutes later, which wouldn't have been unusual except for the fact that, having nothing to do, I was dawdling, driving about thirty miles an hour. Of course it could have been a little old lady on the way to visit a friend at a rest home, but this was not likely, since little old ladies don't tend to drive Hummers.

When the road started curving around a hill I saw that there were in fact two Hummers, coasting along one after the other. I sped up—not much, just a little past the speed limit—and both of them kept pace with me.

I didn't try and lose them. I had more chance of finding out something that might be useful to me if they made a move.

I approached a traffic light that was turning yellow. I decided to stop at it, like a law-abiding citizen. I wanted to see what they'd do.

This is what they did. The lead car sped up and swerved around me and cut me off at a diagonal and the back car came up right behind me so I couldn't back up.

When violence is about to threaten, the worst mistake you can make, I've found, is to assume that you don't have time to think. Acting without thinking is the definition of panic. You almost always have at least a few seconds to evaluate the situation—to assess your opponents and to assess your own resources. When violence is about to threaten, you need to slow yourself down for a moment and think.

As Underwood got out of the lead car and two other men got out of the car behind me, I took a moment to think, and the first thing I thought was that I was an idiot for not bringing along my gun.

Underwood had brought his.

"Get out," he said.

The second thing I thought was that maybe I should try some fancy driving: back up fast and smash into the Hummer behind me and jerk the wheel and—but my car was tightly pinned.

"Get out," Underwood said.

The other men had their guns out too. One of them I didn't recognize; the other was the gatekeeper—Charlie Chaplin.

I considered just keeping my windows rolled up and calling 911, but between them they could have left my brain well ventilated before I got past the 9.

I got out of the car.

"Rev," I said to Underwood. "Charlie," to the other guy.

"Reporter," Underwood said. "You're a reporter."

"Ink-stained wretch," I said. "Breezy, fast-talking newshound."

"It's funny," Underwood said. "After you left I looked you up on the Internet. Couldn't find any of your bylines."

"Well that's because I have a pen name."

"You sized up Dr. Frye pretty good," he said. "Any time a member of the media comes around, the doctor gets so excited he creams in his pants. So all you had to do is tell him you're a reporter and he'll tell you everything you want to know. But you're as much of a reporter as I am. Not everybody in the Party of God is a moron, unfortunately for you."

"Thanks for clearing that up for me," I said. "I was wondering."

"It was a mistake for you to come all the way out to the country, Hymie," Underwood said. "You're a long way from Jewville out here."

"Jewville," I said. "That's good. That's really good."

Underwood still had his gun trained on me.

"See what he's carrying, Teller," he said.

Charlie Chaplin moved up behind me and started taking things out of my pockets. I didn't have anything much for him to take. I thought about spinning around and taking his gun away and grabbing him by the throat and twirling him like a Raggedy Ann and holding him in front of me and using him as a shield and shooting Underwood and the other guy—but the odds of that working out didn't seem so high.

"Twelve dollars," Charlie said. I heard my wallet drop to the ground, twelve dollars lighter. "No gun."

"No guns," Underwood said. "You travel stupid and you travel light. Let's see what else you have."

He came forward and patted me down and found the death threats I'd shown to Frye.

"What the fuck are these?"

"They're letters that were sent to Andrew Carpenter. Maybe you wrote them."

"I don't have any pen pals named Carpenter. I don't know what the fuck you're talking about."

"He's a doctor who received a few death threats from your organization, and who then, coincidentally, ended up dead."

"Never heard of him," Underwood said.

"Really? I was thinking you might be the one who killed him."

"I don't know what you're talking about, Jewboy. I know the names of everybody I've killed, and I never killed anybody named Carpenter. But I might kill you."

Charlie had his gun in my back.

This situation, by the way, provides an illustration of the fact that real life is different from the movies. If a private detective in the movies is confronted by three bad guys, the odds are woefully stacked against the bad guys. There's no self-respecting private eye in movieland or TV-land who can't fight off five or six men without breaking a sweat. And if the bad guys happen to have guns, that's just a trivial detail. The good guy can disarm them all, and will be in danger of suffering nothing worse than a flesh wound, something he can easily laugh off.

This is not the way the world works. You can't laugh off a bullet wound. I knew a man who bled to death after being shot in the leg. And no matter how tough you are, if you are alone and confronted by three bad guys who have the intention to hurt you—well, the smart money would have to go with the bad guys.

I admit that I was scared. Private detectives on TV or in the movies are never scared, even when people are shooting at them. But in real life, I don't know if it's humanly possible *not* to be scared when someone is pressing a gun into your spine. Unless you're a psychopath.

Underwood tossed the letters to the ground and put his gun in his belt.

"If you move your head," Underwood said, "my friend will blow a hole through it."

I didn't say anything. I didn't have any wisecracks left in me.

The barrel of Charlie's gun was still in my back and I stood stiffly at attention as Underwood examined my face judiciously—he looked like a painter scrutinizing a canvas, looking for the perfect spot to put the dab of paint that would add the finishing touch to his masterpiece. Then, evidently having found the spot, he brought his arm back and, guiding his fist carefully, he punched me in the face.

It was an awkward blow, but it did its job. I staggered backward a step, and I felt something hit me sharply at the base of my skull. The punches were not quite simultaneous, but they were close. I had never been punched in the face and the back of my head before. I ended up on my knees.

"Got anything to say now, Jewboy?" Underwood said. I was on the ground. It was dusty. I had dirt in my mouth.

"I didn't think so."

Underwood knelt next to me and grabbed my hair and pulled my head up.

"I'm not going to kill you today, Jew, because Doctor Frye just gave a sermon the other day about embracing more sophisticated methods. But if you're stupid enough to cross my path again, I will kill you instantly. Your thoroughly pathetic life won't have time to pass before your eyes. So stay away."

Underwood and Charlie got in their cars and drove away. I had a nice view of their shoes as they retreated from where I lay on the ground. I picked myself up a little while later, retrieved the letters, got back in my car, and drove back to the city.

To the untrained eye, it might have appeared that I had failed to control the situation.

# Chapter five

I guess I oughta see the other guy," Kate said. Kate was a young woman who worked for me a few days a week, paying my bills, sending out invoices to clients, keeping things organized.

This evening, in addition to her usual duties, I had sent her out to buy a slab of raw sirloin steak, which I was now applying to my blackened, bruised eye.

"Actually, the other guy doesn't look so bad. I mean, he's ugly. But unscathed."

"Well, that's the difference between you then. Next week you'll be handsome again, and he'll still be ugly."

"Thank you, Kate."

Kate had been working for me for about six months, and sometimes I still found it hard to believe my luck. She was one of the smartest, quickest people I'd ever met, and one of the nicest, one of the most good-hearted. She was getting her MFA at the New York University Creative Writing Program, and she'd responded to a classified ad I'd placed looking for a part-time secretary. She'd once showed me a few pages of something she'd written, and I thought they were brilliant. I was under no illusions that I'd be able to keep her for long: she was headed for bigger things. But I was lucky that she was working for me now.

"If you wanted me to," she said, "I could put a little foundation on you, and nobody'd even know you had a black eye. I'm very good with make-up."

"I didn't think you used make-up."

"I rest my case," she said.

I was mad at myself. I'd underestimated my opponent, which is the most foolish thing you can do. I thought I could just bop up there, shake up the rubes, and find out everything I wanted to know. It would have cost me nothing to bring my gun, but I'd thought I wouldn't need it. I'd been too cocky.

"So did they do it?" she said. "Did they kill Carpenter?"

"I don't know yet."

"Well I think they did," she said.

"Why?"

"Because they're evil. They want to send African Americans to Africa and Jews to concentration camps and women who've had abortions to hell, and they sent death threats to Carpenter, and as soon as you came around asking about it they tried to scare you away. Which of course they could never do, but they don't know that."

"Maybe. I don't know, though. It doesn't smell quite right to me."

"What do you mean?"

"I'm not sure."

"You're gonna have to give me more than that, Singer, if you expect me to solve this case for you."

She was joking, but not completely. Although I'd been working in this field for fifteen years and she had been temping for me for fifteen weeks, when I thought out loud about a problem in her presence, she often got to the answer faster than I did. She had a knack for this. I knew she would have made a great detective, but I had never told her that. It's not a life you wish on somebody. It's not a vocation anyone should take on unless they absolutely *have* to.

"So what comes next?" she said.

"A little research, a little snooping around, maybe a little breaking and entering. The usual."

"Can I help out with the breaking and entering?"

"You can help out with the research."

"How come you never let me get involved in the fun stuff?"

"You could get hurt. And you have more important things to do in your life. You have promises to keep." I opened up the bottom drawer of my desk. "Could you get me a glass? Two, if you're thirsty."

Kate reached over to the shelf behind her and got a glass. "A private eye who keeps a bottle of whisky in his desk drawer. How does it feel to be a cliché?"

"It's cream soda, actually." I opened the twist-off cap carefully so I wouldn't spill any soda on my desk, tapped out a couple of Advils from a bottle I kept in the top drawer, and drank. "And now I have to go home, lie down, and let this slab of meat do its work."

After I got home, I put some ice in a plastic bag, found a CD of Bach's Solo for Cello in D Minor, pressed play, lay down, and put the bag on my eye. I'd put the raw meat in the refrigerator. It had mostly been for the purpose of impressing Kate. It doesn't do anything that a bag of ice can't do better.

# Chapter six

Donald Ellis was a little bit crazy. He had enlisted in the army in the 1960s in order to go to medical school—Uncle Sam paid his way—and he'd done his first two years of doctoring in Vietnam. The medical work performed by a doctor who's near the front lines, of course, is mostly butchering: the only tools that Ellis really needed there were saws, for amputating, and tourniquets, for staunching the flow of blood. In the thirty-five years since then, Ellis had worked at the New York University Medical Center, but you got the sense that he still missed the good old days. That was why he worked in the Emergency Room: it was the only kind of doctoring that simulated the conditions he'd known in Vietnam. I'd met him in the late 90s, when I came into the ER one night with a bullet in my side. He seemed to think I was a sissy because I wanted an anesthetic. "That's not the way we worked in the field," he'd told me at the time. "We saved the painkillers for recreational uses."

I thought that he might be able to tell me something useful about Carpenter, so we arranged to meet for breakfast at a coffee shop near NYU. Ellis was already eating when I got there. I ordered coffee and scrambled eggs.

"How you been?" Ellis said. "You're looking pretty well."

When I'd shaved that morning I could barely see out of the swollen purple lid of my left eye.

"I'm looking well, am I? What kind of doctor are you, man? Don't you have anything to say about this thing?"

Ellis briskly cut a slice of ham and shook his head. "I thought I'd better not say anything. Out of respect. For you. That's a pretty sad excuse for a black eye. Whoever did it never learned to throw a punch. I figured you must have gotten into a tiff with one of your girlfriends. I didn't say anything because I didn't want to embarrass you."

I should have known he wouldn't be concerned about my eye. I don't know why I'd even bothered mentioning it. The thing I liked about him as a doctor, actually, was that the only health problem he took seriously was death itself. He seemed to think that nothing else was worth getting excited about.

"So you have a black eye. Big deal. You want me to kiss it and make it better?"

"Okay, I get it. Forget I ever mentioned it."

"Now you're talking sense. So what do you need? What do you want me to tell you about Andrew Carpenter?"

"Anything you can tell me that might help shed light on whether or not he was murdered. And why he was murdered, if he was."

"Murdered? I thought it was a hit-and-run."

"Not everybody thinks so."

"Who doesn't think so?"

"There's such a thing as gumshoe-client confidentiality, my friend."

"Oh. Sorry. Well, I'm sure he had his share of enemies. He was an arrogant son of a bitch. But every hotshot doctor is an arrogant son of a bitch."

"He was a hotshot?"

This was just a way of asking Ellis to tell me more about him, but Ellis seemed annoyed at my stupidity. "Of course he was a hotshot. He was the head of pediatric surgery at the foremost hospital in New York. You think they give those jobs to the interns? And don't let the 'pediatric' fool you into thinking he was a cuddly bear of a man. Pediatric surgeons are the coldest bastards of all."

"Why is that?"

"Any good surgeon is cold. Surgeons lose patients sometimes. It doesn't matter how good you are; it just happens. Michael Jordan didn't used to nail every jumpshot, and even the best surgeon doesn't nail every case. But when you move on to the next patient, you can't sit around moaning about how if only you had done this thing and that thing different, you could have saved that other patient's life. It's true for a pediatric surgeon just like it's true for any other surgeon. But if you're a pediatric surgeon you have to work even harder to be cold, because you're cutting up kids. You could really go nuts if you thought too much about your mistakes, or if you thought about them in the wrong way."

"What does that mean? Thought about them in what wrong way?"

"I mean you think about them, because you don't want to make the same mistake twice, but you don't, you know, dwell on them. You need to analyze your mistakes, but you can't let yourself sit around crying about them."

"Okay. So Carpenter was cold. What else can you tell me about him?"

"People go into medicine for a lot of different reasons. Out of a desire to help people, out of intellectual curiosity, out of the desire to have a decent income. And maybe all of us, at the bottom of it all, have some desire to play God. But with Carpenter, I always got the feeling that the desire to play God was the main thing."

"What made you think that?"

"The way he held himself, for one thing. You always knew he thought he was the smartest guy in the room. He probably was the smartest guy in the room, most of the time, but there was a certain kind of pleasure he took in letting people know it."

"What else?"

"He liked embarrassing other doctors. The head of pediatric cardiology here, Bill Rodney—very nice guy—always used to refer his toughest cases to Carpenter. And Carpenter had a way of making the families feel that Rodney had messed things up. He made them feel that Rodney had sent them over just a little too late. He let them know that he, Carpenter, was gonna save their kid, but it was gonna be a lot harder than it might have been, because Rodney had taken too long to refer them."

"Was Carpenter right?"

"No. When Rodney thought a kid needed Carpenter's services, Rodney sent them along right away. There was never any delay."

"I heard that Carpenter might have made some enemies with a right-to-life group," I said.

"Well, of course."

"Why of course?"

"He was doing stem cell research. Everybody who does stem-cell research makes enemies with right-to-life groups." Ellis took a sip of his coffee and looked uncharacteristically reflective. "That's how you can tell if a man is any good or not. If he makes the right kind of enemies."

"Don't get all philosophical on me here, Doc."

"Don't call me Doc."

I only called him Doc because it annoyed him.

"But from what you're telling me, it sounds like he must have made enemies all over the place."

"Carpenter? No doubt about it. He made a lot of doctors look bad."

The more enemies he had, of course, the harder my job was going to be. I had been hoping that Carpenter had had no enemies in the world except for the Party of God, but that hope was now officially out the window.

I had no more questions to ask Ellis, and I knew he hated small talk, so there was no further reason for us to be there. I called for the check.

"Oh, one last question," I said. "You were saying that people go into medicine for all sorts of different reasons. What was your reason?"

"I just like to cut people," he said.

# Chapter seven

Every time I'd ever seen Clarence Lincoln, he'd been wearing a three-piece suit. I had the feeling that in the unlikely event that I were ever to see his baby pictures, he'd be wearing three-piece suits in those too.

Lincoln was the executive director of the Democracy Project, an organization that monitored the activities of hate groups and tried to combat their influence by means of education. The group was not well-funded, but through the sheer force of his personality, Lincoln had given it an air of distinction. A few hours after I had breakfast with Donald Ellis, I met with Lincoln at his office in midtown. The hallways were quiet and radiated an aura of calm seriousness of purpose.

"Singer," he said, at his office door, extending his hand. "It's been a long time. You look as if you've been in of those highly cerebral arguments you tend to get into. Other than that, you're looking well."

Lincoln himself was looking well, but then, he always was. He was a slim, elegant black man, about six feet tall; he had a way of commanding a room without saying a word, when he wanted to. His signature suits always looked as if they had just been pressed.

He had once explained to me that in an age of hip-hop, an age in which young black men wore pants that slid down their backsides to emulate older black men in prison (who wear their pants that way simply because they're not allowed to wear belts), he thought it was important to demonstrate that a black man can be radical in his actions without being thuggish in his deportment. When he'd told me this, he had gestured toward a series of photographs on his office wall, photographs taken during the early days of the Civil Rights Movement. He had pointed out to me that the young people, white and black, who had integrated luncheon counters all across the South, had all been dressed respectably, and that the men in the crowd during the 1963 March on Washington, the march that culminated with Martin Luther King's "I Have a Dream" speech—black and white, young and old—were almost all in suits and ties. "If you're going to fight the powers that be—to fight them seriously, rather than just make your dissent a posture, an act, a temper tantrum—then a sense of personal responsibility is essential. And one way to demonstrate that—a small way, but not an insignificant one—is by dressing in a manner that implies that you respect yourself and you respect the people you're dealing with." After he'd told me all this, he'd smiled, a small smile, and added: "This is why, in your language, I've always thought it important to look like a mensch."

Lincoln was not a man for small talk. After I sat down he said, "How can I help you, Nathaniel?"

"I've been asked to look into the death of Andrew Carpenter. The pediatric surgeon at Sloan-Kettering."

"I never knew him, but I know the name."

"And I was wondering what you could tell me about the Party of God."

"You believe they were involved?"

"According to his wife, they sent him death threats. Because of his work with stem cells."

I took out copies of the notes and put them on his desk.

He put on his reading glasses and examined them carefully.

"You can't rule anything out," he said, "but if these were authentic, it would surprise me."

"Why?"

"Not their style. Not their style at all."

"Do you mean they tend to use spell check?"

He smiled. "Yes, that's the dead giveaway. There are some hate groups that use spell check and some that don't, and the Party of God...." He looked at the notes again. "No. Seriously, it simply doesn't seem like their style. To my knowledge they haven't been involved in any violence, and although groups like this can often mutate, there's no reason I can think of that would explain why they would be mutating now. Their management has been stable for some time. Arthur Frye has been running the show in a pretty steady manner since he assumed control. He's actually been taking them in the opposite direction: their beliefs are the same but their style is far smoother and more corporate than it used to be. And as far as I know their funding profile hasn't changed: they're still getting their support from the same sources. So, although, as I say, we can't rule anything out, there's no obvious reason why a group that until now has left the violence to its more activist brethren should all of a sudden want to get involved in anything like this kind of crude harassment, let alone murder."

"Could it be some other hate group that wants to hide behind the Party of God?"

"Could be. Could be anything. But I doubt it. That's something I've never seen. I've seen right-wing hate groups commit crimes and then deny responsibility, but I've never seen one of them try to pawn off the responsibility onto another one. One right-wing hate group sending death threats in the name of another right-wing hate group...it just doesn't sound right."

"Yeah. I agree. It sounds too complicated."

"If you could connect Arthur Frye with a crime, however, it would be a glorious day."

"Why is that?"

"How much do you know about the recent history of the Party of God?" he said.

"Not much. I've read a few things about them and looked at some of their literature."

"Let me fill you in. The Party's founder, Ray Stangle, died about a year ago. No one expected Frye to assume control. But he's an exceptionally clever man. He outmaneuvered the faction that everyone thought would take over after Stangle died."

"Would that be a faction led by the Reverend Jonathan Underwood?"

"You've done your research."

"Actually, I met the Reverend." I touched my eye. "My research got a bit physical."

"He gave you that?" He seemed amused. "True to form. Underwood is a born-again psychopath, and I was truly hoping that he would take over the helm. If he had, the Party of God would have been discredited in six months. Arthur Frye is a much more dangerous man."

"I met Frye. He didn't seem dangerous to me."

"That's his genius. He's much more dangerous because he's much more cunning. He's much more dangerous because he's much more smooth. The story of American politics over the last fifty years is the story of how the right wing has become smoother and more intelligent. And unfortunately that applies to right-wing hate groups as much as to every other part of the right. Twenty years ago you had the Christian Coalition: Jerry Falwell, Pat Robertson, Jimmy Swaggart—all those fire-breathing, Bible totin', certifiable maniacs who eventually scared so many of the American people that the Democrats were able to take back the White House for a few years. But the right became cannier, and that means they became slicker, more soothing, so that the firebreathers were succeeded by people like Ralph Reed—the man who took over as head of the Moral Majority from Falwell. A very smooth operator, baby-faced, respectful, respectable—someone you could take home to introduce to your Jewish grandmother. The story of recent American politics is that the madmen have found ways to appear mainstream. The Party of God is no exception. In five years, it won't even be called the Party of God anymore. I'm sure of that. It'll be called the Party of Principles or something—and it will be a hundred times more sophisticated and a hundred times more dangerous."

"So you'd say I'm barking up the wrong tree here. They're not likely to have killed him."

"That's right. It's true that the religious right has been fighting stem cell research. But organizations like the Party of God have been fighting it in the smartest way possible: electing a president who shares their views. That's the level they're moving at today. The death threats are too crude, too vulgar, and, most important, not a fraction as effective as what they're actually doing. Why would they bother to waste their time with murdering a doctor?"

"It sounds like you're right."

"So where does that leave you in your investigation? What do you do next?"

"I probably keep investigating the Party of God."

He looked puzzled. "Why is that?" he said.

"It does sound like I'm barking up the wrong tree," I said. "But right now, it's the only tree I've got."

# Chapter eight

It was about seven at night when I got back to my office. Kate was at her desk in the reception area, typing on her laptop.

"What are you up to?" I said.

She wasn't doing anything for me. She'd already done everything I'd asked her to do that week.

"I've been working here lately. On my writing. I hope that's all right."

"It's all right with me, Kate. But why do you want to work here? Is this the most convenient place for you?"

"I can't work in my dorm. My floor is filled with twenty-four-hour party people. I usually work in the library. I can go back there, no problem, if you'd rather I didn't work here."

"No. That's fine. It's kind of nice to have you working here, actually."

"How's the Carpenter thing going? Have you solved it yet?"

"Not yet."

"Where do things stand?"

"Carpenter was a man who'd pissed off a lot of people."

"That makes things more complicated. Yes?"

"Yes. It does."

"Too bad. But your friends from the Party of God were among the people he pissed off? Right? So they still might be the people who did it?"

"It's possible. It's starting to sound as if this really wasn't their M.O., but it's still possible."

"So what do you do now?" she said.

I shrugged. "Go home. Catch up on some paperwork and then go home."

"That's a good idea, Singer. Go home. Go home and make some toast."

"Toast," I said.

"Toast. Toast and cocoa. Always helps me think."

"Thanks for the tip, Kate."

I went to my desk and spent some time answering emails and putting my files in order. Kate was working quietly in the outer office. She opened my door and poked her head in just before she left.

"I've got a dinner date with my cousin," she said. "I thought I might come back and work some more later. Will you still be here?"

"I'll probably be gone."

She smiled at me.

"What?" I said.

"That black eye kind of suits you," she said. "It makes you look more…detective-y." And with that she closed the door and left.

I knew what she was talking about. I'm about six two, so I don't exactly look delicate, but I have a face that looks more suited to a Talmudic scholar than a private eye.

In fact, people who knew me when I was a kid thought that I was going to end up as a scholar of some sort. And that's what I thought myself. In college I was an English major; I intended to go on to become a professor of Romantic literature, or even a poet. I started grad school, and got a part-time job as a researcher at a detective agency to pay the bills. It wasn't a job I went looking for; it was just a job I stumbled into after a couple of days of looking through the help wanteds. One week in the middle of the winter, after I'd been working there a few months, two detectives, two of the guys who did the actual legwork, got sick with the flu, and the owner, Mike Ferruci, threw me a case that involved going out and talking to people. Ferruci found that I was good at it, and he promoted me out of the research room and made me a field investigator—a real detective. And I found out that I liked it: I liked helping people, and I liked the glamour (which turned out to be purely imaginary, but imaginary glamour is better than nothing). And I liked the sheer strangeness of the fact that I, a Jewish kid from Jersey with a literary bent, was working in a tough-guy profession. I worked for the Ferruci agency for a few more years, and then, on my thirtieth birthday, I decided to go out and start an agency of my own.

When I moved out of the research room and started working as a real detective, I realized that I was going to have to change a few things about myself. At the time I was pretty much a pacifist. I still am—when I think of politics, at least, the people I admire the most were pacifists. Martin Luther King and Gandhi had more balls than any other political figures I can think of, and, despite the fact that pacifism is always dismissed as impractical, they accomplished a lot more than anybody else has in the last hundred years. But if I was going to succeed in my chosen profession, I knew I'd have to learn to use my fists. So I became as fanatical about self-defense as I had been about learning Romantic poetry during college. I took karate, aikido, jujitsu, and kenpo. Then I cut out the bullshit and learned how to box. I boxed for ten years, mostly getting my ass kicked by kids who were younger and meaner and hungrier than I was. I wasn't troubled by the fact that I didn't win too often, because being in the ring was just a sport: on the rare occasions when I needed to use my fists for real, my buried streak of insanity always kicked in. When two guys are fighting, it's usually the craziest one who wins—the one who fights as if he doesn't have anything to lose. And somehow I've always been able to fight that way.

The fact that I don't look very "detective-y," as Kate put it, has usually been a help, not a hindrance. The bad guys tend to underestimate me. Despite the fact that I don't look the part, and despite the fact that even after fifteen years of doing it I still sometimes shake my head in amazement at the fact that life has brought me to this vocation, I can't imagine doing anything else. I feel like it's what I was made for.

When I left the office that night, instead of going home and making toast, I drove up to 54$^{th}$ Street and 8$^{th}$ Avenue. I had a couple of calls to make at the Midtown North Precinct.

Midtown North is one of the oldest police buildings in the city. It was built in the mid-1870s, around the time the city was beginning to expand uptown, beyond the confines of Greenwich Village. It must have been a magnificent structure back in the day, but now it was a hulking, gray monstrosity.

The third floor of the building is the home of the labs and research facilities, such as they are. All of the offices on the floor have a shabby and under-funded look. I was visiting a lab technician named Parikh.

When I opened the door of his office, he didn't look up. He was sitting in front of a petri dish, peering into it intently. In his right hand he held some small precision instrument and was manipulating the substance that was in the petri dish; in his left hand he held a club sandwich.

I was already in the room, but I knocked on the door anyway, out of politeness. He still didn't look up.

I knocked again, louder.

It wasn't that he was hard of hearing; it was just that he was absorbed in studying his evidence. This was a quality I admired in him. He had a faculty of absolute concentration that I envied.

I went in and sat down next to him. I decided not to say anything, just to wait until he noticed that I was there. It only took five or ten minutes. When he finally found what he was trying to find, he lifted up his head, nodding with satisfaction.

"Hello," I said.

"How long have you been here?"

"I just got here," I said. I didn't want to embarrass him. "What have you got for me?"

"A little bit. Not too much."

I'd sent Kate to Parikh's office the day before to drop off the death threats that had been sent to Carpenter—the original letters, and the copies that I'd shown to Frye and Underwood.

The chair Parikh was sitting in had wheels; he pushed his desk and sent himself rolling over to a file cabinet, from which he extracted the letters.

"It was hard to get anything from the originals. They were handled by a lot of people: Carpenter, Mrs. Carpenter, undoubtedly a few members of New York's Finest who weren't quite competent enough to put on rubber gloves before they started mauling the evidence. From the copies, I get your prints and two others, fairly clearly."

"Those would be Frye's and Underwood's."

"I checked both of them against my database, and neither of them is in it. So neither of these people have criminal records. Now, I'm sure that one of them doesn't match any of the prints on the original letters. But the other just might. I can't tell for sure, but it might."

"Can you show me?"

He put the two letters, the original and the copy, beneath a machine of the kind used for reading microfilm. The images were then projected onto his computer. He moved the cursor to one set of fingerprints.

"This is one of the gentlemen whose prints you obtained yesterday. As I said, it doesn't match anything." He moved the cursor to another. "This is yours. No known criminal activity." Then he moved it to a third set. "These prints are the ones that might match up with one of the fingerprints on the original death threat. I can't be sure, but they might."

It was at the top of the page. The top of the page had been handled by Underwood.

"Thank you."

"I wish I could have given you something more conclusive. But

I can't. Fingerprinting is one third science, one third art, and one third myth. Lie detector tests, of course, are completely myth. If you ever have the time and interest, and feel like treating me to lunch one day, I can explain it all to you in detail. But right now all that you have to know is that the fat-thumbed individual who handled the upper left quadrant of this missive just might be your man."

Parikh sometimes talked like someone who had spent too much time alone.

I thanked him again, and then I went downstairs to see Keller. He was at his desk, eating a Subway sandwich.

"I just had an interesting conversation with Parikh," I said.

"My favorite lab rat. How's he doing?"

"How should I know? Has he ever talked to you about his personal life?"

"Never. Not once. I've known him for almost ten years now, and I still know nothing about him. I once heard a rumor that he's married, but I have no idea."

"That's the beauty of Parikh," I said.

"Anyway, what did he tell you?"

"I got some fingerprints from the two bigshots at the Party of God yesterday. One from the brains and one from the muscle."

He looked up at me, for the first time since we'd started talking.

"It looks like you got more than just fingerprints. It looks like you got some knuckleprints too."

"Yeah, that too."

"So here's what I can't understand. You told me that you guys looked into the death threats and decided that his wife'd probably written them herself. But in the meantime they had fingerprints on them that weren't hers and weren't her husband's. It turns out that they might belong to somebody from the Party of God. So this is my question. Are you guys real cops, or just pretend cops?"

Keller, as I've said, was a good guy. A lot of people in his position would have thrown me out of the building—called me an outsider, called me an amateur, called me a Jew, called me whatever. Instead, he looked properly embarrassed.

"It wasn't my case," he said. "But that isn't really the point, is it? It sounds like we missed a few steps."

"Whose case is it?"

"One of the best guys around. That's why I'm surprised. It was Lee Macy's case."

I'd never met Lee Macy, but I knew who he was. He was older than I was—he must have been in his forties—but he had the image of the perpetual golden boy. He was a star. He was one of the smartest detectives on the force, one of the quickest to close out his cases. He was much admired, both within the force and in the outside world. He got quoted in the papers a lot. Even liberals liked him. The *Village Voice* had once run a profile of him in an article titled "Five Good Cops."

From what I knew of him, he was a little too slick for my taste. From my point of view, his high profile didn't speak well of him. The truly good cops aren't getting profiled in the *Village Voice*. They're giving everything they have to being good cops; they're not spending any time making sure people know how good they are. If policemen had PR agents, Macy was a policeman who would have one.

"It sounds like Macy should be spending a little less time reading his clippings and a little more time on his cases."

A short dumpy guy dressed in street clothes with a gun on his belt—another detective—was walking past Keller's desk with a mug of coffee in his hand. He gave me a Who-the-hell-are-you? look.

"Why was Macy working this case, anyway?" I asked. "Isn't he still on the West Side?" Carpenter had been killed on East 68th Street.

"Yeah, he's still on the West Side," Keller said, "but sometimes we have to go out of our jurisdiction. You want to know why? Because we don't have enough manpower. And you want to know why we don't have enough manpower? Ask your friend David Dinkins."

Keller had suddenly turned unpleasant. I wondered whether it was because I'd been overheard talking trash about Macy. He was probably afraid that he was going to be accused of fraternizing with the enemy.

"My friend David Dinkins?"

"You're a liberal, aren't you? You must have voted for him, right? So if you have some problems with the fact that the police in this city are spread too thin, that's who you should speak to."

It was probably true that the police force didn't have enough manpower. It wasn't true that Dinkins had anything to do with it. His one term as mayor had ended more than ten years earlier. But since he was black, and a liberal, a lot of cops found it convenient to blame everything on him. Fifty years from now, when New York City cops are grousing about how the city doesn't do enough to support them, they'll still be blaming it all on David Dinkins.

## Chapter nine

After I left the police station I checked my messages and found that Mrs. Carpenter had called to ask if I'd learned anything. Her voice sounded shaky. I called her back and arranged to visit her at her apartment.

She lived on Fifth Avenue, on Museum Mile—just north of the Met, just south of the Guggenheim. The doorman who let me in wore a pained expression, as if it bothered him that I was using the front door rather than the service entrance. I took the elevator to her apartment, which was the penthouse. It was one of those arrangements where the elevator opened to only one apartment.

She met me at the door. She looked as if she hadn't eaten or slept since the last time we'd met. She had a drink in her hand.

"It's good of you to see me," she said. "I don't imagine you've had time to find out anything much."

"No, I haven't. I've really just started asking around."

"Goodness." It had taken her a second to register my black eye. "Is that what happens when you just start asking around?"

"This? No. This is from an old friend who dropped by to let me know he was back in town. Just his way of saying howdy."

Since I didn't have any news for her yet, I didn't think it served any purpose to let her know that I had indeed gotten beaten up while trying to find out what had happened to her husband. She would have thought, incorrectly, that I must be hot on the trail of something. Underwood had probably just beaten me up for fun.

"Sounds like you have lovely friends," she said. She smiled and looked into my eyes, making a visible effort to brighten. I imagined that when she was truly happy, her smile could have lit up a room. Not just a room—if there had been some way to harness it, it probably could have solved the problem of the U.S.'s dependence on foreign oil. But now, though her smile was a lovely smile, it was a lovely sad smile.

"Can I get you a drink?" she said.

"No. Thank you."

"Something non-alcoholic, then? We were always entertaining. I think I have just about everything here."

"Club soda would be fine."

"An ascetic," she said. "Or a recovering alcoholic. Or both. One club soda, coming up." She disappeared into the kitchen.

She came back with a club soda for me and what looked like scotch or bourbon for herself.

"I'm not really sure why I asked you here," she said. "I knew that the odds weren't high that you would have found anything out yet. I'm probably wasting your time."

"Don't worry about that. You're my client, and I'm happy to check in with you whenever you want."

Actually, I *was* worried. I had once lost a client in a similar situation: a woman who was left so distraught by the death of her husband that she swallowed a bottle of sleeping pills. She had wanted me to meet with her once a day, and I'd blown her off, because I was busy looking into her husband's death. I thought she was just being a nuisance. At the time I was too young to understand that what she wanted was simply a feeling of reassurance, a feeling that somebody was on her side.

"It's been very strange," she said. "I feel at loose ends, for the first time in my life. I'm sure I'll get over this, but…for the time being, I just feel very disoriented."

"You've suffered a great loss, Mrs. Carpenter. It's only natural that you don't feel like yourself."

"Thank you," she said. "But it feels a little more strange than that. I'd like to believe that I'll eventually feel like myself again…but the problem is that I'm not sure what 'myself' is. I married Andrew when I was twenty-two. I was just out of college. My ambition in life was to be a teacher. I wanted to teach kindergarten or first grade. I was enrolled in Bank Street, to get a Master's degree or a PhD in elementary education, and I took classes for a year, but then things started to move so quickly with Andrew's career that it made more sense for me to stay home and help him out. Andrew was young and handsome and personable and obviously on the way up, so the hospital wanted to showcase him, and then when he started to make breakthroughs in his field, he was in even more demand, as a fund-raiser, as a lecturer. I was the only person who was really capable of organizing his life. It was like I had a full-time job, and an important one. I was part of something that mattered. And now I'm part of nothing. And I have no idea what to do with the rest of my life."

I didn't know what to say. I didn't know what she should do with her life either. I grunted, in a manner that I hoped would sound sympathetic.

"In the first week after he died," she said, "everyone was very kind. People kept coming over, people kept bringing food. I couldn't bring myself to eat anything, but it was nice that people were bringing it. It made me feel cared for. I was surrounded by people all day. But it's all getting harder now. People have stopped visiting. Andrew was loved by a great many people, but even for them, life has gone back to normal. His death has become just another story to tell at a party. But for me it's not a story to tell. It's the only story. My life can't go back to normal. There is no normal anymore. My life was with him. My life *was* him. I have no life anymore."

She stood back up and went into the kitchen and poured herself another drink. Then she went back to the couch, bringing the bottle with her this time so she wouldn't have to get up again. She was walking unsteadily, yet somehow she still had an air of stateliness and grace.

"I do believe that my husband was murdered, Mr. Singer. But I suppose a change has come over me in the two days since I encountered you. I think I believed that if you could find out what happened to my husband, then I would somehow feel better. From the day when I realized the police weren't going to help me, until the day I met you, I fixated on the idea of finding a good private detective. I could think of nothing else. And then, after I found you—after I *found* a good private detective—I realized that even if you did find out what happened to Andrew, it wasn't going to help me at all. I would still be a woman whose life had been taken away from her. Even if you confirmed that it was a murder and you brought the murderer to justice, I would still be a woman who had built her entire life upon the foundation of her love of one man, her partnership with one man. And now that that love is gone, now that that partnership is gone, the life is gone as well."

When we are in mourning, of course, our grief feels everlasting. It's impossible to imagine that things will someday be different, be better. This might have been the moment for me to reassure her that she would find another foundation, on which she'd build a new life. But although I thought it was probably true, I wasn't sure—I'd known people who were so devastated by the death of a spouse that they never made it all the way back—and I didn't like to traffic in shallow reassurance.

"I'm wondering whether you would like me to stop working on the case," I said.

"Why do you ask that?"

"My services are expensive, Mrs. Carpenter. It sounds as if you may have discovered that the services I offer aren't really what you need right now. If I understand what you've been saying, and finding out the truth isn't going to bring you the relief you were hoping for, then maybe I shouldn't be taking your money to find out the truth."

"You don't want to be profiting on the grief of a woman in mourning. Thank you for being so ethical, Mr. Singer. But I wasn't implying that I was seeking to get out of our arrangement. It's true that I've come to think that bringing Andrew's killer to justice is not going to bring me any feeling of relief or even closure. But that doesn't mean that I want to give up on the effort to bring his killer to justice."

"I just wanted to be clear."

"I appreciate your scruples, Mr. Singer. Please call me when you've learned something about Andrew's death."

"I'll call you in a day or two whether I've learned anything or not. Just to keep you apprised of what I've been doing."

"Just to check up on me, you mean. To make sure I'm all right."

I finished my club soda and stood up.

"I can see why Susannah Parker told me you were a good man," she said.

My clients often tell me that I am a good man, and I always have a mixed reaction when they do. Of course I try to be a good man, and of course it pleases me when people think that I am. But I have refined my life through a process of violent simplification, to a state in which I am nothing but what I do, nothing but my job. It is easy to seem like a good man when you have withdrawn almost completely from normal human engagement. Was I a good father to Wini? Was I a good father to Jack? And if the answer to these questions was no, then could I be called a good man?

But these were questions that didn't concern her. I thanked her, and left.

## Chapter ten

Ithe wat was late when I got back to my office. There was a light under
the door. Kate was burning the midnight oil, working tirelessly on
the Great American Novel. I let myself in.

The thing about Kate, though, was that she probably didn't
have much of a left jab. Unlike the man who greeted me when I
opened the door. He welcomed me with a short, precise punch to my
solar plexus. It knocked me against the wall and took the wind out
of me. After he hit me, he didn't move. He just stood there, observ-
ing me with a look of contempt.

"Hello, hotshot," he said. "My name's Lee Macy."

Getting hit in the solar plexus is no fun. First of all, you can't
breathe for a minute or so. And second—this might be even worse—
when you do get your breath back, the stopped-up oxygen rushing
up your throat causes you to bleat like a sheep.

This had happened to me once or twice before, so I knew that
if I clamped my jaws shut and, when I got my breath back, breathed
through my nose, I could at least avoid the bleating part. This seemed

important, maybe just because it was the only thing about the situation I could control.

I was shaken up, and I felt stupid, and yet I didn't feel afraid. I'd been hit with a punch thrown by someone who knew what he was doing. It wasn't the kind of punch you throw to hurt someone seriously. It was the kind of punch you throw to humiliate someone. It was the kind of punch you throw to introduce yourself: to make it clear to a new acquaintance that you're tougher than he is.

Doing everything I could to preserve my dignity, I slid or slumped my way down to the couch. He sat down in my chair, behind my desk. I didn't like that.

"I heard you knew how to handle yourself," he said. "But, as the man said, I must have been misinformed."

"Make yourself at home," I said. I was still trying to get my breath back.

"I tried," he said. "Cream soda?"

"There's scotch in the cabinet."

He got up and got out the bottle and a glass. He was a shade shorter than I was, with a military-style crewcut and a carefully pressed suit. The muscles of his arms and shoulders were bunched and thick.

"Single malt," he said. "Not bad." He took some ice from the mini refrigerator near the bookshelf and dropped it into the glass. Then he sat back down and put his feet up on the desk. "You've been going around saying unkind things about me," he said. "I don't like that."

"You have the Andrew Carpenter case and you didn't do anything with it. It looks to me like you've done your best to bury it." It hurt to talk.

"Keller told me you were pretty good. So the question in my mind was: why does a private eye who's supposed to be pretty good waste time treating a hit-and-run as if it was a homicide? I could only come up with two possibilities. One is that Keller was wrong, and you're crooked, and you're getting into the business of fleecing widows. If I end up deciding that that's your story, I'm going to kick your ass, because I don't like crooked cops. The other possibility is that since Mrs. Carpenter is one of the tastiest pieces of tail a guy like you is ever going to get close to, you're hoping that if you string her along for a while, she might throw you a blow job or two. If I end up deciding that that's your story, I'll wish you luck, though I might decide to kick your ass anyway, because the last thing I need is some Jewboy wannabe tough guy telling people that I haven't been doing my job."

When you're dealing with cops, you're never on a level playing field. Maybe Macy could kick my ass, and maybe he couldn't. But if it ever reached a point where we had to find out, the problem was that if I kicked *his*, he could come down on me with the full weight of the law—assaulting an officer can bring you twenty years, even if all you did was slap him—or, if he preferred, with the sheer lawlessness that only lawmen can command. I once knew a private detective who beat up a cop in self-defense, and two days later received a midnight visit from a plurality of the membership of the Greater New York Chapter of the Policemen's Benevolent Association, and who, three years later, still can't hear a thing out of his right ear.

"So Macy. Tell me something. If you're as good as everybody says you are, how come you told Keller that Mrs. Carpenter manufactured those death threats herself? It took me less than a day to find out that the secretary treasurer from the Party of God left his fingerprints on the letters."

I wasn't being technically accurate here—all Parikh had told me was that there was a chance that the fingerprints on the note were Underwood's—but I wanted to see what he'd say.

"Keller says I told you that?"

"That's what he said. Was he wrong?"

"First rule of being a detective. You might want to write this down. Don't believe what you're told when you're talking to a moron. Keller's been a burnt-out case for the last ten years, and even in his better days he was never too bright. I told him I checked into the Party of God and they didn't have anything to do with it. They're holed up there in Nyack or whatever, issuing their declarations about the end of the world, and maybe one of them gets excited and puts a few letters in the mail to spook a few liberal doctors. But they didn't murder him. Murder isn't their thing, and even if it was they wouldn't have done it that way. If you want to kill somebody, you make sure to get it right. Running somebody over is the least efficient way there is." He was about to go on, but then he shook his head. "Shit, you know all this. If you're worth anything, you know this. You know this, you know I'm right, but you're going around saying you have a problem with me. And the only way to explain why you're doing that is that you want that nice piece of ass up on Fifth Avenue to think that there's some reason to keep paying you. You tell her the cops screwed up but you're going to fix it, but that it's going to take some time. Is that it?"

It was true that Keller was a burnt-out case, but it wasn't true that he was stupid. If Macy had told him that he'd looked into the death threats, Keller would have remembered it. He wouldn't have gotten it wrong.

But I agreed with what Macy was saying about the Party of God. They weren't likely to have killed Carpenter, and if they had, they wouldn't have killed him this way. "I didn't tell her I was going to fix anything. All I told her was that I was going to look into it. It's one of the things that a private detective does. Take another look at a case the cops might have been too busy to take a close look at. You know that, Macy. I do it a few times a year. Usually I find out that the cops did a good job in the first place, and there's nothing more I can do. Once in a while I find out that the cops missed something, and I end up helping out. This case is different than the others, though. This is the first time I've had a cop come around crying to me about it, because I'm making him look bad. What's up with that, Macy?"

By putting it that way—"crying to me about it"—I was trying to insult him: I was telling him he was a wuss. I wanted to bother him.

I succeeded. He was out of the chair very quickly. I stood up, ready to punch him in the teeth, but he drew his gun, which led me to reconsider. He put the barrel of the gun under one of my nostrils and he pushed, so that my head was tilted back against the wall.

"This is one of the things I like about Jews," he said. "You all got such big noses that I can put the barrel of a .38 inside it very comfortably."

I didn't say anything. It's only on TV that people get mouthy with somebody who's holding a gun. In real life, it doesn't happen.

"You can look into it all you want, Hymie. You can string the widow Carpenter along for long enough to put your grandchildren through college, for all I care. But if I ever hear of you disrespecting me again, I'm going to be back, and that cute little secretary of yours is going to be scraping your brains off the carpet. Or maybe you'll be scraping her brains off the carpet. It all depends on what mood I'm in."

After he left, I double-locked the doors and slid the chain lock in place, but I was still feeling rattled.

The thing that bothered me the most was what he'd said about Kate. She was working for me because she'd needed a part-time job and had answered an ad I'd placed on Craig's List. Now somebody was threatening her life.

I sat there trying to calm myself down and to find a way to profit from my meeting with Macy. Trying to learn something. What had I learned from this?

I learned that Macy had some stake in the Carpenter investigation—that he had some stake in making sure that no one started looking into it. I didn't buy the idea that he was just a proud cop, ticked off because he'd heard I was disrespecting him. No cop is that proud. When you work in law enforcement, people call you the worst names they can think of, all day. You get used to it.

I made a cup of tea and did some more thinking. There was just one other thing about Macy that stuck in my mind. Not the kind of thing you think about when somebody is pushing the barrel of a gun up your nostril, but the kind of thing you think about later.

He was awfully well dressed. It was one of the most impressive suits I've ever seen. I have a couple of banker friends, old money, people who get their clothes hand-tailored from Italy or Hong Kong, and the suit that Macy was wearing wouldn't have been out of place in their closets.

The question I had to ask myself was: How does a cop afford a suit like that? It seemed impossible. Impossible for a clean cop, at least.

## Chapter eleven

I was making coffee the next morning when Kate arrived.

"You're not supposed to be here today," I said. She worked for me three days a week.

"It's nice to see you, too," she said. "I told you that I'd like to do my own work here once in a while, if it was okay with you. And you said it was okay."

"Yeah, I did."

"And I left the other day before I could finish organizing your receipts. So I was planning to finish that up and then spend a few hours on my own work. So let me finish making that coffee for you, big guy, and then I'll get out of your way. If any damsels in distress come in and ask for you, I'll show them in."

A few days ago, when Kate had said she'd like to do her own work in my reception room, it had sounded fine to me. More than fine. I didn't harbor any romantic feelings for Kate—she was too young for me, and anyway I didn't want to mess up her life—but that didn't stop me from feeling a small but definite thrill every time I saw her. I enjoyed her because of who she was—a brilliant, large-hearted, high-spirited young woman—and I enjoyed her because of what she represented. To me, she represented the possibility of getting life right. She hadn't made any big mistakes with her life yet; she hadn't compromised her talents; she hadn't seen her spirit wasted away in fruitless relationships with the wrong men. She had a shot at finding fulfillment in both love and work.

So it was usually a joy to have her around. But not now.

"You know, Kate, actually, I'm thinking that it might be a good idea if you didn't come here for a while."

"What's the matter, Singer? You can't concentrate while I'm around? What's distracting you? Is it my beauty or my brains?"

"That's the problem, Kate. I can't figure out which of them it is, and I keep turning it over in my mind."

"No. Really. What's going on? From the moment I walked in the door I could tell something was bothering you."

I told her about Macy's visit. She listened closely. She had a wonderful, full-souled way of listening.

"That sounds scary," she said, when I was through.

"It was. And that's why I'm thinking it would be better if you stayed away from here for a while. It would be better for you, because it would be safer. And it would be better for me, because I won't have to worry about you. So I'll be able to concentrate on the case."

"I appreciate it that you want to look out for me, Singer. But on the other hand, to hell with you."

"How's that?" I said.

"Every once in a while, at the end of the working day, I tell you fascinating stories from my life. Haven't you been listening? My father was a Green Beret, and I spent my first fifteen years in Fort Bragg and Fort Dix and Fort Charlton, and whenever he was away on some assignment, overthrowing some democratic government somewhere, which was most of the time, most of what I did every day was fight off these asshole Special Forces guys who wanted to kiss me."

"I know that you're as tough as they come, Kate. But Macy doesn't want to kiss you."

"Life involves risks, Singer. I know that. Working for you

involves risks. You told me that the day I interviewed for the job, and honestly I've been surprised at how peaceful everything's been so far. I've given a lot of thought to how I want to live my life, and I know that I don't want to spend my life running away from risks. You've made your own choices about how to live, and my guess is that they haven't always been the choices that the people who cared about you wanted you to make. But if they really cared for you, they didn't try to change you. They respected your choices. So please do me the favor of respecting mine."

I thought about this for a while. Then I opened a desk drawer and tossed her the envelope of receipts that she was supposed to organize.

"Well, get to work," I said.

# Chapter twelve

I called Parikh and asked me if he could get hold of the file on Carpenter's death. I didn't call Keller. I was pretty sure he would have given me a copy of the file if I'd asked him, but I didn't want to put him in jeopardy. Though I wasn't happy admitting it to myself, Macy had frightened me. I intended to keep poking around into the Carpenter business, and I didn't know what Macy would do about it. I was afraid of what he might do to Kate, and, although Keller and I weren't friends, particularly, I was also afraid of what he might do to Keller.

Parikh was an anonymous guy in an out-of-the-way department; I doubted that Macy even knew who he was. So I wasn't afraid I'd be putting him in danger by reaching out to him.

I spent the rest of the morning setting up appointments to talk to people who'd known Dr. Carpenter. This took a while. A lot of them didn't want to talk to me, so the process involved a lot of back-and-forthing. I called them; they said no; I called Mrs. Carpenter's assistant, who got in touch with them and told them that Mrs. Carpenter hoped they'd cooperate with me; I called them again; and most of them ended up agreeing to meet with me. I could have had Kate do all this but I wanted to get some first impressions.

As I was doing all this—the glamorous work that takes up about ninety percent of a detective's time—I was trying to figure out how I could find out more about the Party of God. By the time the afternoon rolled around, I had an idea.

I rented a car and drove up to Nyack. My own car worked fine, but Underwood and Chaplin and the other guy knew what it looked like, and having them spot me wasn't part of my plan. I waited within sight of the front gates of the building. I had a couple of books to pass the time. One of them was a collection of essays by Schopenhauer; the other was a book about the forging of currency.

The Schopenhauer book was the one I wanted to read, even though I only understood about one out of every three sentences he wrote. I thought his basic view of the world made sense. To the extent that I could understand him, he believed that life consists of little more than suffering, and that if we believe we can escape this destiny, we're deluding ourselves. His only prescription is that, because all of us are fellow sufferers, we should have compassion for one another.

But the forgery book was the book I actually read. I didn't have any particular interest in the subject or any particular reason to be reading the book, but one reason that I'm good at what I do is that I make a constant effort to keep informed about every subject that could possibly have any bearing on my work. It's like being in graduate school perpetually. There might be some time when the knowledge of currency forgery comes in handy. Burrowing inside books was one of my skills, and my habit of devouring every bit of information I could get on every subject related to criminology, even subjects related only in the most tangential way, had come in handy more than a few times in my career.

A little past five, people started leaving. It wasn't until five thirty or so that I saw the person I was looking for: Frye's secretary, Amy Roth.

She drove out of the parking lot in a Toyota Corolla. A very sensible vehicle. I followed her, making made sure to keep a few cars between us at all times. I assumed that the odds that she'd be able to pick up a tail were slim to none, but it's not wise to take such things for granted. Early in my career I visited a loan shark to get him to lighten up on a client of mine. The loan shark lived with his grandmother, a genial old lady who introduced herself to me and then went back to watching *All My Children*. I went into the loan shark's office to try to get him to listen to reason, but after a few minutes our conversation got a little spirited, and his grandmother, in a touching display of family feeling, entered the room with a Berretta and starting firing warning shots at my head. Luckily her aim was shaky, but she taught me a lesson I would never forget.

I followed Amy over the Tappan Zee Bridge and into Tarrytown, a quiet suburb on the Hudson River. She parked in the driveway of a small two-family home.

I waited a few minutes—gave her time to change her clothes, have something to drink, wash up, feed her cat, whatever. The considerate detective. Then I rang her doorbell.

People are trusting in the suburbs, even people who work for organizations who believe that the country is secretly being ruled by a Zionist-Communist conspiracy. She opened the door all the way before she knew who it was.

"Oh," she said.

"Hello. I see you remember me. I was wondering if we could talk for a little while."

"Talk about what?" She put her hand on the door. She looked as if she was considering slamming it in my face. Since I might well be an agent of the Zionist-Communist conspiracy and all.

I didn't try to force my way into her apartment, because I didn't want to frighten her, but I came forward a little bit, so that if she did decide to slam the door, slammage wouldn't be possible.

"I had a few questions that I didn't have a chance to ask the other day. I thought you could help me. I didn't want to bother Dr. Frye again. I'm sure he's a very busy man, with very important matters to deal with."

She softened. She obviously considered Frye a great man, so

she appreciated how solicitous I was about wasting his time. Perhaps she also was gratified that I had given him a doctorate.

"Of course, I could have called Reverend Underwood," I said. "But just between you and me, I got the feeling that the Reverend wouldn't be too helpful. I'm not sure how such a thing could be possible, but I even got the feeling that he wasn't fond of me."

I don't know how to put a twinkle in my eye, but I gave it a try as I said this. On the day I visited their office I'd gotten the powerful impression that she didn't like Underwood—when he and I were snarling at each other she'd looked amazed that I was taking him on, and she didn't look unhappy about it. So I was trying to conjure up a sort of mischievous, co-conspirator feeling between the two of us. The smooth-talking detective.

"I really only have a few questions," I said.

She hesitated, and I had the sense that several different impulses were at war inside her. Her loyalty to her organization and to Frye made her think it would be a mistake to talk to me. But she didn't like Underwood, and she probably wanted to talk about him with someone who liked him even less than she did.

"I'll talk to you," she said. "But just for a few minutes. And not here."

When I'd visited the Party of God the other day, I'd been a journalist. Underwood knew it wasn't true, but of course I had no idea whether he'd told anyone else. It didn't matter, really. Journalist, private detective, whatever I was, Amy was evidently willing to help me.

She agreed to ride with me in my car (people are trusting in the suburbs) and directed me to a restaurant one or two towns north. She said that it was a place she went to often, and she never ran into anyone she knew there.

As I drove, she gave me directions, but, for the first few minutes, she didn't say much else. Finally, though, she said, "Can I ask you something?"

"Anything."

"What happened to your eye?"

My eye had looked much better in the mirror that morning. It was no longer scary-looking, but it was still purplish and puffy enough for her to notice it.

"That's how I know that the Reverend Underwood wasn't fond of me," I said.

When we reached the restaurant she ordered a hot chocolate and I ordered coffee. Then the waitress started hassling us about the minimum, so I ordered a chop steak. When I cook for myself at home I never eat meat, but if you're a private detective on the job it's generally a mistake to order a veggie burger. A certain element of machismo is an asset in this line of work, a quality that becomes harder for you to project if you make the mistake of putting the idea of tofu in people's minds.

"So, Mr. Singer. Now we're here, and there's probably enough caffeine in this hot chocolate to keep me up all night. So I hope this is important. What can I do for you?"

"I'm not sure if you heard the conversation I had with Dr. Frye."

"A little bit," she said. She seemed embarrassed to admit this. "I didn't mean to eavesdrop, but you were right next to my desk when you were speaking with Dr. Frye."

"Then you know that I was concerned that a doctor in New York who died last month had gotten death threats purporting to be from the Party of God."

"I understood that much. Yes."

"I know that Dr. Frye is above reproach. But honestly, I have to say I have my doubts about Reverend Underwood."

She was looking down into her hot chocolate.

"I have a feeling," I said, "that you think my doubts are justified."

She took a sip from the cup, put the cup back in the saucer, and then dabbed at her lips with her napkin. She still hadn't looked at me.

"I have a feeling that you know the Reverend Underwood is

capable of reprehensible acts. I have a feeling that this troubles you a great deal."

I was fishing. I couldn't tell if I was reaching her at all.

"I can understand why you feel hesitant to talk about it with me. You don't want the reputation of a good organization to be tarnished. You don't want to see any damage done to a good cause."

She still hadn't looked up.

"But deep in your heart, I think you know, Amy, that if Reverend Underwood isn't stopped, he is going to do far more damage to the cause than any outsider could do. If the Reverend Underwood isn't stopped, he could destroy the organization."

All this was coming out of me through sheer intuition. I would speak a sentence without any idea of what I was going to say next, gauge her reaction, and speak the next sentence.

"I don't think he was ever a good man. But I think he's become an evil man. I think he's embraced the darkness." She said this in a whisper.

He's embraced the darkness. It sounded as if she was describing Darth Vader. I waited. After a while I said, "When did things change?"

"Things changed when Dr. Frye became the director. Dr. Frye has wonderful ideas. He's changing the organization in beautiful ways."

"And the Reverend couldn't stand that," I said. "The Reverend is trying to hold on to the old ways."

"The Reverend always believed that when Dr. Stangle passed, he would inherit the leadership of the party. I always prayed that it wouldn't happen. I always prayed that the Lord would intervene so that Reverend Underwood never did take over. When Dr. Frye joined the organization, my prayers were answered. Everyone saw that his way was the way of the future. Everyone except the Reverend, and a few of his friends."

"I've heard nothing but good things about Dr. Frye. You won't be surprised to learn that I don't share your organization's beliefs, but

I know that the doctor is a man of unimpeachable personal integrity."

I knew nothing of the sort, of course. But when I said this, she looked at me as she hadn't looked at me before. She put her hand out, as if she wanted to clasp mine, and then demurely withdrew it.

"I'm so glad to hear you say that. *I* know it's true, but it's always difficult to tell whether people who are not among the faithful can see it too. My sister always tells me I'm crazy. She tells me that the only difference between the doctor and Reverend Underwood is that the doctor is more well-spoken. But I know that isn't true. I know that *can't* be true. I can't tell you how much it means to me to have you, an outsider, tell me that he sees things the way I do."

Her face was glowing with gratitude and relief. I felt an immense sadness. I have known others like her. People whose impulses are good, but who are so naïve, so filled with yearning for a wise father figure, that they become eager pawns for the worst causes. The politics never mattered. Amy Roth belonged to a lunatic army of the extreme right, but she could just as easily have belonged to a lunatic army of the extreme left. If she had been born in a different time, she might have ended up a Weatherman, placing bombs in buildings where innocent children slept, in the deranged conviction that indiscriminate killing would usher in the socialist revolution.

"Can I tell you something you might not believe?" she said.

I nodded.

"I was hoping you would find me. When you showed up at my door I wasn't completely surprised. I was hoping that you would visit me and tell me that you knew that there's something wrong with Reverend Underwood."

"You only met me for two minutes," I said. "Why were you hoping that?"

"Because you didn't seem afraid of him. I think you're the only person I've ever met who didn't seem afraid of him."

I don't think this was a testament to my fearlessness. I think it was a testament to the way the bigshots in a cult can create an atmosphere in which the members are in awe of them and outsiders are strictly barred from entering.

"I really don't know if anyone in the Party could have done the things you said. Sending death threats, or really…killing anyone. I hope not. But I do know that if anyone could have done them, or ordered someone else to do them, it would be Reverend Underwood." She was speaking in a tense whisper. "I think the Reverend is out of control."

"He *is* out of control," I said.

She took a long breath. "I feel like I've been waiting for you to come along. For years. I feel like I've known what I have to do, but I needed someone to come along from the outside. To help me see that I was right. And to help give me courage to do it."

"What do you mean?"

"I've known, for a long time, that the Reverend isn't a good man. Sometimes I think he's an agent of Satan, sent to destroy the Party of God from the inside. But I've never been able to talk about it with anyone. If I told anyone inside the Party, the Reverend would find out, and he'd have me expelled. Or worse."

"You said that you needed courage to do what you need to do. What are you talking about?"

"I can stop him," she said. "I've known for a long time that I can stop him. But I need help."

"How can you stop him?"

"I have information. I have information that could put him in jail for a long time. I don't have information about any murders. I don't know if he's committed any murders. But I have proof about bad things he's done."

"What kind of proof?"

"Letters he's written. Notes he's made."

"Why haven't you ever acted before, Miss Roth? Have you spoken about this to Dr. Frye? Or to the police?"

"Dr. Frye is too good a man to see what the Reverend is doing. When your heart is pure you can't see the evil intentions of others. I don't think he would believe me. And the police…. The police around here are all part of the Reverend's old boy network. They're his friends."

"Tell me about some of the bad things he's done."

"He's bribed people. And blackmailed."

I wasn't sure I believed this. I was beginning to be afraid that Amy Roth was paranoid. That her devotion to Dr. Frye was so deep that she had begun accusing Underwood of imaginary crimes.

"Why did he do these things? For money?"

"He did them all for power. For power in the organization. A lot of people who don't like him, who are loyal to Dr. Frye, have been driven away. He can't challenge Dr. Frye directly, but he's doing everything he can to undermine him."

"Who did he blackmail?"

"He blackmailed Daniel Brown, Dr. Frye's executive secretary. He was very close to Dr. Frye. Daniel Brown's son did something very bad, and the Reverend Underwood found out, and he used the knowledge to make Mr. Brown leave the organization. He wanted to weaken Dr. Frye."

"And all this has been going on without Dr. Frye noticing?"

"Dr. Frye is concentrating on spreading the word. He is doing such important things that he doesn't see any of this."

"And you can prove these things?"

"I can." She lifted up her chin with a look of defiance. "Nobody notices me. I'm not sure that the Reverend Underwood even knows my name. But sometimes being a wallflower can give you an advantage. You can observe people without their realizing they're being observed. You can see where they've put things. You can make copies of things. You can notice when they're too lazy to use the paper shredder."

"If you give me copies of everything you have, I can help you. I can help the Party of God become as pure as you and Dr. Frye wish it to be."

"Bless you," she said—first time I'd ever been blessed—and this time she did clasp my hand. "I think the Lord must have sent you to us for a reason. I've hidden the things in a safe place. I didn't want to have them in my home. I can get them for you as soon as Saturday."

"Shall we meet on Saturday night, then?"

"I would love that. That would mean so much to me."

She was so overcome by emotion that she let me buy her another hot chocolate.

"I'm afraid this will keep me up all night," she said. "But I'm in the mood for celebrating."

She'd said that she didn't have any information about any killings. But of course she might not know what she really had. The information she'd collected about Underwood was a kind of thread. If I followed it, there was no telling where it might lead me.

As I drove her back to her apartment I thought about how I had felt it so important to protect Kate. I'd even thought it was important to protect Keller. Lying to Amy was one thing; putting her in danger was another.

"I should let you know," I said, "that you might be exposing yourself to some risk. After you give me your proof, I'll do everything I can to make sure that the Reverend never finds out where it all came from. But I can't promise that he won't find out, one way or another. The police might subpoena you as a witness. Or he might figure it out on his own."

"So what are you saying?"

"I'm saying that it might be wiser for you not to stick your neck out."

"Thank you," she said. "But I want to stick my neck out."

"I just need you to understand that that may not be wise."

"It may not be wise. But I still have to do it. I don't have a choice."

"Why is that?"

"I haven't been lucky enough to have children, Mr. Singer. But I have a niece. She's more precious to me than anyone in the world. And I've talked to her about how important it is to stand up for what you believe in. I've talked to her about how important it is to be brave, and not let anyone intimidate you out of doing what you think is right. I know that this could be dangerous. But if I didn't stick my neck out, I'd never be able to look my niece in the eye again."

"I can't argue with that," I said.

"Maybe it will all work out," she said. "I've been hoping that someone would come along who could help bring Reverend Underwood to justice. And now here you are. Maybe you're the answer to my prayers."

"Let's hope so," I said.

# Chapter thirteen

When I got to my office the next morning, a copy of the police file on Carpenter's death was already on my desk. Kate, ever efficient, had stopped off at Midtown North and picked it up from Parikh.

It read like a textbook on how not to conduct an investigation. After the accident, or whatever it was, the cop on the scene had spoken to several witnesses and taken down their phone numbers and addresses. In a case like this, it was standard police procedure to follow up by re-interviewing the witnesses a few days after the original interview. It's done to confirm the original reports—to make sure the cop on the scene didn't get anything wrong—and to find out if any more details have emerged in the witnesses' memories. The follow-ups had been done by Lee Macy. But they were the laziest follow-ups I'd ever seen. There were five eyewitnesses, and he hadn't gotten anything new, not one memory, from any of them.

When you reach Macy's rank, you don't necessarily have anyone looking over your shoulder on a case like this. So you have the authority to close a case without doing any work on it at all. As far as I could tell, that's just what Macy had done.

When I'd pointed out to Keller that the Upper East Side wasn't even in Macy's jurisdiction, he'd said that Macy could have caught the case because of a manpower shortage. I didn't believe that. Someone of Macy's rank gets to pick and choose. But why do you pick a case if you're not going to do any work on it?

※

I spent the rest of the day doing follow-up interviews—doing them properly, the way Macy should have done them. The only improper thing about them was that I led the interviewees to believe that I worked for the police department. I didn't exactly lie to them. I didn't actually *say* I was from the police department. But I did mislead them. I told them I was a detective doing follow-up interviews on the hit-and-run, and of course they all assumed I was from the police department. They had no reason to doubt it.

I talked to three of the five on the phone. I did get a few details that hadn't found their way into the police report, but nothing that seemed likely to matter. I was beginning to think that Macy had gotten all the information there was to get. Maybe he did follow-ups as well as anyone else did, and just had a lazy way of writing them down.

The fourth eyewitness, a man named Matt Marino, insisted that I see him face to face. "I can't stand the goddamn phone," he said, "so if you want to know what I have to say, you're going to have to get your ass out to Bay Ridge."

I got my ass out to Bay Ridge in the early afternoon. The Brooklyn Bridge is one of the glories of New York, but once you get over the bridge, you're in a landscape remarkable for its ugliness. Many years ago, Walt Whitman wrote about "Brooklyn of ample hills" and the "beautiful hills of Brooklyn," but Whitman's Brooklyn was no longer in evidence. Parts of Brooklyn sometimes made me think that alongside our yearning for beauty, humankind has an innate yearning for ugliness, a need to create and live amid horrible surroundings. It was these parts that I drove through on my way to see Matt Marino.

The small block he lived on was not part of the general squalor, and his house radiated a sense of pride of ownership. It was a one-family house, with a small lawn which was so carefully manicured you could believe that the owner cut it with a pair of scissors. I rang the bell and a man in a wheelchair opened the door.

"You from the law?" he said.

"Mr. Marino?" I said. "Nathaniel Singer. We spoke earlier. I'm a detective looking into the death of Dr. Andrew Carpenter."

That seemed to be an answer to his question, although it actually wasn't, so he let me in.

He was a man in his thirties, with a bulky, overdeveloped upper body and thin, wasted legs. He was wearing purple shorts and a T-shirt that read, "Hey Osama: Kiss my ass!"

"The law, the law, the law," he said to himself as he wheeled himself down the narrow corridor toward the living room. We passed a bedroom and I took a glance. On the floor there was a set of free weights; on the wall there was a rack of hunting knives and a rack of rifles.

I was walking behind him. He started talking to himself in a scornful singsong. "I fought the *law*, and the law put me in *awe*. Don't jaw at the law, or the law will find your flaw."

I was beginning to tense up a little. Crazy man with rifles and knives. Not good.

"Sit yourself down," he said. "Make your ass at home. You want something to drink? You want a beer? I got Sam Adams. You want something stronger? I got Johnny, I got Jack, I got any fucking thing you want."

"No thanks."

"What's up with that? Don't drink on the job?"

"Not too often."

"A very responsible dude? Or a total wuss? Let God be the

judge. Let's see. I got some Gatorade. Does a wuss like you want some Gatorade?"

"That's all right. No thanks."

"Red Bull? You ever drink that shit? It tastes like piss, but it does the job. I like to have a couple of cans before the ladies come by. It puts a little shimmy in your jimmy, if you know what I'm saying. Never needed shit like that before the accident. I used to fuck the wife all night and then drive over to the Gowanus Canal and pick up a couple of those twenty-dollar hookers and get a couple blowjobs. Two from each hooker. They used to give you a deal in those days if you got more than one blowjob."

On one wall of the living room were pictures of Marino and his wife: a pleasant-looking chubby woman with a sweetly goofy smile. In all of the pictures, Marino was standing, or sitting without a wheelchair. On another wall were photographs that had been cut out of porno magazines.

He already had a glass on the coffee table. He picked it up and drank from it. "Red Bull and rum. That's what I've been flying on lately. Red Bull and rum."

I took my notebook out and put it on his coffee table in front of me. "So you were on the street when Dr. Carpenter was hit."

"Sure as shit was. Sure as shit was. I'd just come out of the hospital. I'm up there twice a week for rehab." He bent over in his wheelchair and lifted one of his legs. "Look at these things. Both of them limper than Wayne Newton's dick. The doctors say they're going to have me running the marathon someday. The lying little fuckers."

"How much of it did you see?"

"I saw everything. I wasn't watching the doc, but I *was* watching the doc, if you know what I mean, because he was walking with a lady who was one of the tastiest little pieces of quim I'd seen in a long time. Then he said goodbye to her, and I was still watching her shake her sweet little thing, but he was in the corner of my eye. He was out in the middle of the street, and out of nowhere you got this little red sports car that plows right into him at maybe fifty miles an hour and keeps going. The sound it made, man. I once dropped a pumpkin out of a helicopter. That's what it sounded like. You could have had your eyes closed and you still would have known the dude was history. He might have been a hotshot doctor two minutes ago, but now he was just pumpkin pie." He raised his drink to his lips with a fond smile, remembering it all.

"The car that hit him. Did you notice anything else about it?"

I said this as casually as I could, because I didn't want him to see that he had told me anything I didn't already know. Inside I was boiling. No one—not the cop on the scene, not Macy—had written down anything about a red sports car. The instrument of Carpenter's death had been left undescribed: it could have been an Edsel; it could have been a Hummer; it could have been a sleigh pulled along by dancing reindeer.

"Little red sports car. That's what I told your buddies, and that's all I can tell you. I can't tell you if it was a TransAm or a Corvette or a Mustang, because I don't know, and I don't give a shit. I never gave a shit about cars. The kind of guys who were all car crazy in high school were the guys who couldn't get laid. Not me, my friend. Not me. I never had any trouble in that department."

"I think I know the answer to this already, but I have to ask. You didn't happen to get a license plate number?"

"Fuck no. What do you think I am? Matt Marino, boy detective? 'Gee, maybe if I turn in some clues, the mayor will give me a badge and a whistle.' I wasn't looking for the license plate. I was looking at the ooze coming out of the dude's head. I was thinking I wanted to go out to a diner and have me a nice warm plate of pumpkin pie."

Leaning forward in his wheelchair, he looked pleased by his own wit. He reached over a box on the coffee table, took out a cigar, and lit it. "You don't mind if I smoke, do you? Not that I give a shit if you do mind."

"Is there anything else you can tell me, Mr. Marino? Anything you noticed—anything at all?"

"That's about it, Mr. Officer Sir. I noticed that that piece of quim I told you about wasn't wearing any underwear, but I don't know if that would be pertinent to your investigation." He blew a couple of satisfied smoke rings. "And you know how I know she wasn't wearing any underwear?"

I put away my notebook.

"I know she wasn't wearing any underwear because I followed her back to work and we did it in the ladies' room. First time you could say I was forcing it on her, the next two times she was begging for it."

I stood up. "Thanks for your help, Mr. Marino."

I could only guess what had happened to this man. My guess was that he'd lost his wife and his legs in an accident, and that it had unhinged him. But all I really knew was that I was ready to get out of there.

He maneuvered his wheelchair so that he was blocking the corridor. He moved it smoothly, still holding his cigar.

"Aren't you going to ask why I said I wouldn't talk to you unless you came out here?"

"I wasn't planning on it."

"But I want you to know."

When somebody volunteers to tell you something, you should find out what it is. At least you should if you call yourself a detective. But I didn't care what it was. I wanted to leave. Clearly he'd had his tragedies, and maybe he'd been a fine man before whatever happened to him had happened, but that was none of my concern. I didn't like this guy, and I wanted to get out of the sad little swamp of his world.

"I wanted you to come out here because I wanted to let you know how much I hate the cops."

"I'll put that in my report."

"It was the fucking cops that did this to me. You know that already, though. You know that I've got you people to thank for the fact that Mary is dead and I'm a goddamn…vehicle."

"I didn't know that. I'm sorry for your loss, Mr. Marino."

"Sorry for my loss." He was still holding his cigar. Now rolled up his trouser leg and he pressed the lit end against his knee. He didn't take it away. He looked at me steadily. His expression didn't change. After a moment I could smell his skin burning. "You know what it's like to live with this?"

"No. I don't."

"No. You don't. But you might get a taste of it if I was to break both of your legs for you. Would you like a little taste of it?"

"I'm leaving now, Mr. Marino. Please get out of my way."

"You're leaving? How are you leaving? Through what exit? You think you can take me, Mr. Law? I'm on wheels, pal, but don't let it fool you. I could break you like a twig. Look at these arms, you faggot. I could bench-press you, boy. I could bench-press the moon!"

He lifted his arms triumphantly and beat on his chest like a gorilla. He probably spiked his Red Bull and rum cocktails with a generous helping of steroids. The particular flavor of his mania was a dead giveaway.

"You know what?" he said. "You don't have a gun, do you? What a fuck-up you are. What a true fuck-up. You thought you were gonna take a nice drive out to scenic Brooklyn and interview a friendly witness, so there was no need for that big heavy gun. What a mistake, my man. What a colossal fuck-up on your part."

I'm six foot two and two hundred pounds, but who knows?—he probably *could* have bench-pressed me. But on the other hand, as he'd pointed out, he was on wheels. I bent down and seized the footrests and stood up, pulling the footrests up with me, and the man who could break me like a twig, the man who could mess with the moon, was suddenly flat on his back. I stepped around him and out the door. I could hear him cursing at me as I put my key in the ignition of my car.

I was still thinking about him as I crossed the Brooklyn Bridge. I genuinely felt sorry for the guy. I wondered if it was too late for him to fight his way back to sanity. The photographs of him with his wife seemed to suggest that he had once been sane.

My profession has made me keenly aware of how fragile a human life is, how the most well-protected lives can be blasted to smithereens in an instant, leaving nothing but bafflement and rage. I have seen so many people deconstructed by violence and grief that at times human identity seems like a structure built of glued-together toothpicks. We think we're stable, we think we're strong, but under the right amount of pressure, anyone can be smashed, crushed, transformed radically downward, rendered unrecognizable to himself.

I put Marino out of my mind. Being a detective is probably a little like being a doctor. It's a line of work that puts you in constant contact with people's sadness, and you have to find a way to put all that aside and concentrate on the few things that matter, the few things that have relevance to the task at hand. The thing that mattered, in this case, was that I'd found out about a little red sports car.

## Chapter fourteen

The elusive last eyewitness was a man named Glen Dean. I called him from my cell phone, and this time he answered. I told him who I was, in the usual brief and misleading way, and asked if I could meet with him.

"My Gawd, man," he said. "It's about time."

He lived up in Inwood, just north of the George Washington Bridge. I got there a little early and took another look at the reports that Macy and the beat cop had filed. I hadn't been mistaken: there was nothing about a red sports car. Most of the witnesses hadn't actually seen the accident. They'd just heard the sound of it, and when they looked, they'd looked at Carpenter rather than the car.

Dean buzzed me into his building. When I got to his apartment, he was already standing at the door. He was probably in his late sixties.

"Behold the majesty of the law," he said as I came toward him down the hall. "Try not to touch anything in my apartment."

He was a very small, fit-looking man with a trim beard. According to Macy's notes, he was a restorer of antique furniture.

He had an envelope in his hand, and he gave it to me.

"What's this?"

"The bill."

"The bill for...?"

"No one told you?"

"No one told me what?"

"Astonishing," he said. "Astonishing. You're the people who are supposed to protect us? The gang that couldn't think straight."

"We don't always communicate that well with one another in the department."

"Give the man a prize for the understatement of the year," he said.

He let me into his place. His living room was very clean. He had an impressive collection of art from the ancient world: masks on the walls, small statuettes on every surface.

I opened the envelope and found a bill, made out to him, from the Hypnotherapeutic Institute of North America.

"So you're telling me that you don't know anything about this?" he said. "Why are you even here?"

"I told you why I'm here. I'm here to do a follow-up interview, to find out if there's anything we might have missed."

"What's the point of a follow-up interview, though, when the last policeman I talked to couldn't even follow up to the extent of telling you what we spoke about? What do you think you're following up *on?* Why does the police department insist on sending yet another muscle-bound ignoramus to talk to me? Do you have some quota of interviews you have to meet, so you keep sending people around to ask the same questions? Will there be someone else showing up next month to ask me questions that I've already given you the answers to, but that you haven't managed to communicate to him?"

Everywhere I went, I met people who hated cops. I was starting to feel sore about it, even though I wasn't actually a cop myself.

"I have to admit to you," he said, "that I'm seriously miffed."

"I can understand why you're miffed, Mr. Dean. You have a right to be miffed. You also have a right to be peeved, come to think of it. So on behalf of the entire department, I'd like to apologize for the way we've handled this so far. But I'm in charge of this case now, and I can assure you that no information you give to me will be taken lightly, or misplaced, or forgotten."

He seemed mollified by this. "Since you're the first of your kind who's had the decency to be polite to me, I accept your apology. Even though I know that you were having a little joke at my expense with the miffed and peeved business."

"Thank you. I apologize for that too, by the way. Now, it would help if you could explain to me what this bill is about."

"Your colleague, Detective Macy, said the department would reimburse me if I came up with anything that helped. Would you like a coffee or something?"

"Thanks."

His coffee maker was large and elaborate. With its gleaming silver knobs and meshing levers, it looked like a nineteenth-century attempt at a time machine. He removed a bag of coffee beans from the freezer, tapped some of them into a grinder, pressed the top of the grinder to pulverize them, scooped out the grounds very precisely with a measuring spoon, and spread them evenly into a basin in the machine. "It's important not to agitate the grounds," he said. He turned the contraption on, and it did its work with a maximum of noise and steam.

Finally he poured the coffee into a cup and gave it to me. I'm not sure it was worth the effort, but it was pretty good.

"When I spoke on the phone to your colleague Detective Macy, I told him that I had seen the whole thing. I saw the doctor, I saw the car, and I saw the convergence of the twain."

I had started to warm up to the guy, but when he said that I felt like hitting him. I don't like to hear people making fine phrases when discussing the death of an innocent person. The convergence of the twain: it was as bad, to my mind, as Marino talking about pumpkin pie.

"As I told your colleague, I unfortunately didn't see the driver.

I didn't try to get a good look at who was in the car until I realized it wasn't going to stop. I did, however, see the license plate."

"You got the license plate number?"

He put down his coffee cup with an expression of irritation on his face.

"Don't they teach you people basic listening skills? I didn't say I got it. I said I saw it."

"The distinction being that you don't remember it?"

"Now you're getting closer, Mr. Detective. The distinction being that when I talked to your colleague, I couldn't remember it anymore. I was so disturbed by the whole thing that even though I told myself it was important to memorize it, as soon as I thought I'd succeeded in committing it to memory, I promptly forgot it."

"That happens more often than you'd think, actually. You shouldn't feel that bad about it."

"I don't feel bad about it. I feel quite pleased with myself for having had the presence of mind to try to memorize it in the first place."

"Right."

"Well, your colleague seemed to think that that was that. As if once you've forgotten something, it can't be retrieved. I must say, this struck me as startlingly uninformed. Don't they teach you anything about basic brain chemistry in the police department?"

"They actually don't teach us much. No listening skills, no brain chemistry. They just kind of give you a gun and a pair of handcuffs and set you loose on the street."

"No need to be snippy, young man. I'm trying to make a point. When I told your colleague that I thought I might be able to retrieve the memory through hypnotherapy, he acted as if he'd never heard of the technique. I had to give him quite a little lecture about it. He seemed fascinated, especially when I told him about the information from my own childhood that I'd managed to unearth with the aid of a hypnotherapist. By the end of the conversation he said that if I did see a hypnotherapist and managed to retrieve the memory, the department would reimburse me for the cost."

It must have amused Macy to tell this to Dean.

"So Mr. Dean…are you saying that you did retrieve the memory of the license plate number?"

"I wish I were. I'm actually saying that I retrieved a little more than half the number. I'm very sorry. That was the best I could do. I wish it could have been more. But I hope it will be of some use."

"It may be a great deal of use, Mr. Dean."

He went to his desk, opened the top drawer, and produced a piece of paper, on which was written KNG 9.

"Do you remember what state it was?"

"Yes. New York."

"I can't tell you how much we appreciate this, Mr. Dean. It was really very good of you to go to all that trouble. It's rare that anyone will take the initiative like this."

Praise made him glow. He was probably more than twenty-five years older than I was, but since I, as far as he knew, was a cop, I was an authority figure. He looked like a schoolboy whose teacher had just awarded him a gold star.

"Well, thank you. I try to be a good citizen."

"I have one more question. I'm sure it's something you already covered with Detective Macy, but it would be helpful if we could go over it too. Was there anything else you noticed that might be of help? I know you didn't see the driver, but can you tell me anything about the car?"

"I did tell all this to Detective Macy, but since you're being so polite, I have no problem talking about it again. The car was sporty. I think it was foreign. It was bright red. Scarlet, I'd say. And it actually seemed to pick up speed before it hit the doctor."

"Can you say that again?"

"It picked up speed. I'm not sure, because I wasn't actually looking at it until it hit him, but I think I *heard* it, gunning its motor, just before the impact. And I use the word 'impact' for a reason. I'm not going to say 'accident,' because frankly I don't think it was an accident."

"Because the car was picking up speed when it hit him."

"Because of that, and because of the way it sped off. I've never seen a hit-and-run before, but I would think that if it had been an honest accident, there would be a moment of hesitation. The driver would slow down for a second after the impact. But this car just raced around the corner without slowing down for a moment."

I put my notebook in my pocket, stood up, and took out my wallet. "What with all the red tape involved, it'll probably be months before you could get reimbursed for your visit to the hypnotist. So why don't I just reimburse you now." I gave him a hundred dollars, which was the amount listed on the bill.

"You're a good man, Detective Singer," he said. "You've restored my good opinion of the police. You may have even restored my faith in human nature."

After I left I wondered what it meant that his faith in human nature had been restored by a man who was lying to him. It seemed there was a moral problem involved there somewhere.

## Chapter fifteen

On my way back to my office I called Parikh and asked if he could generate a list of people who had license plates that started with KNG. After making it clear that I was bothering him and that he had other things to do and that his job description didn't include responding to endless whims from freelancers, he said he thought he could get me something by the end of the next day.

When I got to my office, Kate was there, sitting in front of her laptop at the reception desk, working on the Great American Novel.

"Remember how you were complaining that the work I was giving you wasn't glamorous enough?" I said. "I think I have something that's going to set your pulses racing." I told her about the list we'd be getting from Parikh. "You're the lucky girl who's going to go through it and see which of the people on it we should take a closer look at."

"What am I looking for?"

"First of all, you're looking for a red sports car. Second, you're looking for geographic proximity. I want to check out people who live in the city or close to it before I check out people who live in, you know, Buffalo. Third, you're looking for anything else that might place them in the Upper East Side on the day Carpenter was killed."

"How do I look for information like that?"

"The same way you'd look if you were trying to track down old boyfriends. Start with Google, and see where that leads you. It won't tell you who has a red sports car, but it'll be a good place to start."

Google has put a lot of detectives out of work. The Internet in general, but Google in particular. People who used to hire trench-coated tough guys to fly halfway around the world to hunt down vanished spouses now just sit down in front of the computer and tap a couple of keys and find out everything they want to know. But for the detectives who remain in business, Google is a godsend. Every detective I know wanted to buy stock in the company before it went public, and was pissed off when the company decided to sell shares by invitation only, to celebrities and other bigshots.

"Before you start working on that list," I said, "do you have the list Mrs. Carpenter faxed over? People she thinks I should talk to?"

"I put it in the file."

"What file?"

"The file on the case."

"We have a file on the case?"

Kate smiled brightly, went to one of the filing cabinets, and produced the file on the case.

"His Girl Friday," she said.

"You're not bad to have around," I said.

"You either. So if you're going to start interviewing people who knew Carpenter, does that mean you're sure you don't like Underwood?"

"Don't 'like' him?"

"You know. Don't you think he's guilty?"

"You've been watching *Law and Order* again, haven't you?"

"Maybe a little."

"Let's keep the TV cop jargon to a minimum around here, if we can," I said.

"Roger that," she said, and smiled at me. It was meant to be a sheepish, guilty kind of smile, but Kate had such a confident personality that sheepish and guilty was something she couldn't pull off. Her smile was simply brilliant, nothing less.

"But you're pretty sure he didn't do it?" she said.

"I don't know. And even if I did, it's a mistake to look in only one direction. You start missing things you shouldn't be missing. Anyway, after I see what Amy Roth has on Underwood, I'll have a better idea of what to do next. I don't want to do anything to disturb the good Reverend until then."

She went to the filing cabinet and got the list. Most of the names were of people who'd worked with Carpenter at Memorial.

I drove up to the hospital and went to Carpenter's office. His name was still on the door. A woman in her late twenties or early thirties was sitting behind a desk, as if waiting for the doctor's next patient.

"Are you Stephanie Winston?"

"That's me."

"My name is Singer. I'm—"

"I know all about you. You're the private dick." She said this in a tone of sarcasm and contempt.

"I don't get it," I said. "I'm employed by the widow of the man you worked with. She's asked me to find out if his death was really an accident or not."

"I know that," she said.

"So what's the problem? Why don't you want to talk to me?"

"I don't want to talk to you because I think you're unscrupulous. Dr. Carpenter walked out into the street and got hit by a car. It was a terrible accident, but it was an accident. But here you are, preying on the grief of his wife, cooking up some lurid little scenario according to which somebody was trying to kill him. You might as well just rob her and get it over with. That's what you're doing anyway, but the way you're doing it is even worse, because you're keeping the wound alive. As long as you're poking around, the healing process isn't going to have a chance to get started."

She delivered this speech without taking a breath. I had the feeling she'd prepared it.

"Maybe," I said, "you should pay Mrs. Carpenter the respect of assuming that she isn't stupid. Maybe you should pay her enough respect to try on the idea that she knows what she's doing, and that she hired me because I know what I'm doing, and I'm not going to poke around a minute longer than I need to. And maybe you should pay her enough respect to believe that she knows how the healing process has to work for her better than you do."

"Whatever," she said. "You're here, and she asked us to cooperate with you, so please just ask whatever you want to ask and then get out of here, and take your little murder fantasy somewhere else."

"I take it that you didn't know that Dr. Carpenter had been receiving death threats?"

This slowed her down, but only for a moment.

"Oh, please," she said. "You're making that up."

"He received three notes from an organization called the Party of God, telling him that if he didn't stay away from stem cell research, they were going to kill him."

She was quiet for a long time. Finally she said, "Do you know when that was?"

"They came within a few days of each other last summer. Just after he was on the cover of the *Times Magazine*."

This information genuinely sobered her. When she spoke again, she spoke slowly.

"Dr. Carpenter was a remarkable man," she said. "He never ceased to amaze me when he was alive, and now it seems that he's going to keep amazing me even after his death."

"What do you mean?"

"There were a few days this summer when he seemed upset. I remember because it was the week after the *Times* article. When I read the article, I thought he was going to be walking on air all week. But he seemed tense. Jittery."

"Did you ask him what the matter was?"

"No. I was surprised, but I just ended up thinking that you

can never anticipate how people are going to react to fame. I think I decided that the publicity made him nervous, and that he was afraid that it might distract him from his work. I remember thinking that that was a little strange, because Dr. Carpenter wasn't normally a man who shunned the limelight. But that was the only explanation I could come up with."

"Why didn't you just ask him what was wrong?"

"We didn't have that kind of relationship. I would never have presumed to ask Dr. Carpenter a personal question."

"Did he say anything at the time…anything that might not have made much sense to you then, but that makes sense now, given what you know?"

"I'm sorry, but there's nothing I can think of. He wasn't that kind of person. He didn't share his troubles with anyone. The only reason I knew he was upset was because he wasn't talking. Usually he had a joke or a kind word for everybody. But there were a few days the week after that article came out that he just came in and did his work and went home. At first I thought it was rude, then I thought he was upset. But I had no clue what he was upset about."

She looked off wistfully.

"It's just like him. If anybody ever thought they could intimidate him with a death threat, they didn't know Dr. Carpenter. His favorite expression was 'Stay the course.' He was not a man who ever gave up."

I gave her my card. "If you think of anything else, I hope you'll call me."

She put the card in her wallet. "This is just so upsetting. When I was sure it was an accident, it seemed like a tragedy. But if it wasn't just an accident, it was so much worse than a tragedy. Think of how different the world might be now if Bobby Kennedy had lived, or Dr. King. In his own way, in his own field, Dr. Carpenter was just as great a man as they were."

I used to know a nice old woman who had two oil portraits in her living room: John F. Kennedy and Jesus Christ. They were depicted in the same gauzy, backlit, idealized way. If you didn't know better, you might have thought they were twins: one of them strait-laced, one of them a hippie. I imagined that if one visited Stephanie Winston's home, one might see an image of Dr. Carpenter above her bed, painted in the same style.

I spent the rest of the day talking to people who had known Dr. Carpenter through his job: doctors, nurses, administrators. Though nobody else actually used the S word, Stephanie Winston's opinion seemed to be universal: the man had been a saint.

Saints, however, as someone once said, should be considered guilty until proven innocent. The more I heard about Dr. Carpenter's unearthly goodness, the more inclined I was to suspect that he must have had enemies I hadn't learned about yet.

I'd been talking to the wrong people. Carpenter had been the head of his department, and all of the people who worked in his department were in awe of him, or afraid of him, or both. With the grants he'd won for his research, he'd brought more revenue to the hospital than anyone else, so the administrators there were nothing but grieved by his death. In the opinion of everyone who worked at this hospital, he wore a halo. If I really wanted to find out what he was like, I needed to start by talking to his rivals.

# Chapter sixteen

Carpenter? Total asshole."

I was in the office of William Rodney, the head of pediatric cardiology at the New York University Medical Center.

"I might not be speaking to you so freely if you weren't a friend of Don's." That was Donald Ellis, my ER doctor friend. "But then again, I might be. Andrew Carpenter was one of the biggest phonies on the planet, and the mere mention of his name can set me off."

"How was he a phony?"

"If you listen to his fan club, his groupies, his cult, whatever you want to call them, he was Jonas Salk and Louis Pasteur and Albert Einstein all rolled into one. And don't get me wrong, he was a great surgeon. But as good as he was at surgery, he was even better at being a bullshit artist. The work on stem cells that he was doing was perfectly good work, but if you look at it closely, his lab was never really making the breakthroughs. Yet somehow Carpenter managed to get his name attached to pediatric stem cell research, almost like a trademark, so that whenever there was an article about the subject, Carpenter was referred to as the leader in the field. Somebody should write it up someday: it would make a fascinating case study in the politics of medicine. The researchers at the Hutch in Seattle, or Minnesota, or Duke—they've always been ahead of him in every area but one. The only place he had them beat was in stroking the press. Two years ago there was a lot of excitement about the discovery that stem cells can regenerate diseased heart muscles in children. The people who actually made the discovery were at the Salk Institute, but you'd never know it from the way it was covered. While they were writing up their findings in the most painstaking, scholarly way, submitting everything to peer review, Carpenter was buttonholing people from NPR and the *Times*. And in the popular mind, to the extent that the popular mind knows or cares anything about these things, he's still considered the person who made the breakthrough."

"Do I sense a little professional jealousy here?"

"Not a bit of it. Research isn't my thing. And I'm not a surgeon. So I wasn't competing with him."

"But if he was the kind of man you're describing, he probably did have his share of enemies."

"Hell yes, he had enemies, but not the kind that'd be likely to run him over with a car. Everybody else who was working in stem cell research hated the man's guts, but he didn't do anything that would make anybody want to kill him. He was a headline grabber and an egomaniac, but that was it. As far as I know."

"Ellis told me that you used to send patients his way."

"It's true. The fact that he was a phony and a showboat and a high-society pretty boy didn't cancel out the fact that he was a great surgeon. In ninety-five percent of the cases that pediatric heart surgeons have to deal with, I have perfect confidence in my staff here. But once or twice a year you get a case that requires someone who's a genius at surgery. When we had that kind of case, I'd send the patient on to Carpenter."

His phone rang. As soon as the person on the end started talking, Rodney looked pissed off.

"No, I have no information about that. You'll have to consult one of the boys on the seventh floor. Yes, I'm aware that nobody requested prior authorization. But you know what? If the same thing happens again, we'll do it the same way. When a kid comes into the emergency room with a blown-out aorta, I'm going to fix it the best way I know how. You think I'm going to call time out and give one of you bureaucrats a buzz and ask you if I'm allowed to use a Salter clip? You really think I'm ever going to use one of those tinfoil things you people have been pushing? Where do you get those things? Out of a Cracker Jack box?" He paused for a minute while the person on the end of the phone was speaking. Obviously it was someone from a health insurance company, unhappy about the fact that Rodney had had the audacity to save a patient's life before figuring out whether it would be more cost-effective to let him die. "Well, that's fine," Rodney finally said. "Dream on."

He hung up the phone. "Bloodsuckers," he said, mostly to himself. Then he looked up at me. "Whenever these managed-care flunkies start threatening me, I know I'm doing my job."

I had been about to ask him something else about Carpenter, but he was staring off, drumming his fingers on his desk, looking as if he was thinking hard. I assumed he was still brooding about the phone call, but it turned out that he wasn't.

"You know," he said, "come to think of it, a year or two ago there were actually some rumors that Carpenter might be a little worse than a headline grabber. I'm not sure I would have remembered it if I hadn't gotten that call from my chum at the insurance company. The only racket I hate more than the insurance racket is the pharmaceuticals racket, and Carpenter, as you probably know, was on the payroll of Weatherall Pharmaceuticals."

"He was a consultant, right?" I said. I'd noticed this on his official resume on the Memorial Hospital website.

Rodney smiled. He looked as if I'd just said something touchingly naïve.

"Yup, he was a consultant. I guess you have to be in the field to have a grasp of the subtleties of the terminology we use. The title 'consultant,' more often than not, is a drug-company synonym for 'whore.' You're a very discreet and very classy whore, but that's what it comes down to. They fly you to conferences all over the world, they give you expense accounts and put you up in the best hotels. You never have to sign an agreement to use their products; you never have to sign an agreement to mention their products in the lectures you give; you never make any commitment at all. But if they've arranged to fly you to a conference to lecture about a certain disease, and if they happen to manufacture a drug that's targeted at that disease, it just stands to reason that you'll mention their drug, doesn't it? It just stands to reason that you'll mention the studies that show how effective their drug is. And if you neglect to mention that there are other studies that cast doubt on the effectiveness of their drug, or that tend to show that some other company's drug is just as good or better, well…. it isn't as if you've actually crossed the line into dishonesty. You would *never* cross the line into dishonesty. You're a healer, a man of science, an upholder of the Hippocratic oath. You're just choosing to be polite to your benefactors, your hosts."

I knew that this thing went on a lot in the medical profession. The Democrats had run some hearings in the 1990s trying to prevent doctors from accepting gifts from drug companies, but of course they hadn't been successful. "But aren't you just saying that Carpenter had his hand in the same till as everybody else?"

"From what I've heard—just hearsay, but from a source I consider reliable—Carpenter went a little further than that. I don't remember the details—I might not have ever gotten the details—but there was something about him pushing a medication before its effectiveness had been proven."

"You don't remember any more of it than that."

"Sorry. I'm drawing a blank. I can ask around and get back to you if anybody remembers anything else. But you can probably ask around as well as I can."

"I have a crack research staff," I said.

"I figured you must," he said. "I figured that's where your profits must go. They certainly don't go into your clothing."

# Chapter seventeen

After I got out of Rodney's office I turned my cell phone on. There was a message from my crack research staff.

"I had a little scare this morning, Singer, that I thought you should know about. I don't want to play the damsel in distress card here, but it might be nice if you could give me a call."

I called her, and the first thing she said was, "I feel so embarrassed that I called you. Forget it. It was probably just nothing."

"I'll be the judge of that. What happened?"

"At about noon I went out to lunch at the Argo." The Argo was a coffee shop on Broadway. "There was this guy who came in a little while after me and sat at the counter. He looked kind of...I don't know...unpleasant. He looked a little like Rondo Hatton."

"Who?"

"That guy who played the Creeper in the old Sherlock Holmes movies. Do you remember the Creeper?"

"I can't say that I do."

"He was a very scary dude," she said. "He's legendary for his scariness, among film buffs. Anyway, about an hour ago, I went down to the Mid-Manhattan Library to look up some stuff for you, and after I left I saw him again. He was standing at a bus stop just outside the diner. When I saw him, he turned his head away. But I'm sure he was looking at me."

My office was on Broadway and 94th Street; the library was on Fifth Avenue and 40th. In other words, they were far apart.

"Lock the door," I said. "I'll be right there."

When I got to my office she was at her desk. She wasn't typing, or researching, or filing. She was just sitting there. She looked pale.

"I feel so foolish, Singer, making you run up here."

"Cut it out, Kate. There was nothing foolish about it. It would have been foolish not to call me. You did the right thing."

She was trying to look strong and unafraid, but it was easy to see that she was relieved that I was taking this seriously. For a second I thought she was going to cry.

"Did he know you made him?" I said.

"Huh?" Kate said.

"Did he see that you noticed him?"

"Is that what that means? I 'made' him?"

"That's what that means. When somebody is trying not to be seen and *is* seen, one says that he was made."

"Where does that expression come from?"

"Jesus Christ, Kate, I don't know. Do I look like Strunk and White?"

"You don't look like White. You might look a little like Strunk, though."

"Kate."

"How come you can ask if I 'made' somebody when I can't ask whether you 'like' somebody? You probably first heard the word 'made' on some cop show too."

"Kate. I'm very impressed with what a tough broad you are, joking around like this when the legendary Rondo Hatton is after you. But we need to focus here. Do you think he saw that you noticed him?"

"I'm not sure, but I don't think so."

"Good."

"Why is it good? What happens now?"

"It's good because it means we have the element of surprise on our side. What happens now is that we'll finish out the workday and you'll head home. Sometime after that, your secret admirer will make another appearance, whereupon I will introduce myself to him. Much to his dismay."

"That's what I was hoping," she said. "I was hoping that when you met him, you would make him feel a certain amount of dismay."

I unlocked a drawer in my desk and took out my gun.

"What's that?" Kate said.

"It's a firearm. It's a .45. Manufactured by Colt Firearms, Hartford Connecticut."

"I know it's a firearm. I know it's a damned gun."

"So why are you asking?"

"It was a rhetorical question, intended to express my surprise. I knew you owned a gun, but I've never seen you take it out before. I've seen you go off to protect people before, but I've never known you to decide you had to have a gun in order to do it."

"No one I've had to protect before has been…you. Extreme affection calls for extreme measures, my dear."

"Thank you. But somehow the fact that you feel the need to bring your gun along makes this situation feel even scarier than it felt a minute ago."

"It's not a scary situation. I'm not taking the gun along because I think I need it to defend you. I'm taking the gun along because once we've met your secret admirer, we'll be asking him to tell us a little about himself, and when someone asks you questions while holding a gun to your head, it has a remarkable way of loosening the tongue."

"It makes a laconic man turn loquacious? Is that what you're trying to say?"

"Precisely."

Both of us were making such a show of using fancy language because we wanted to mask the fact that we were nervous.

At five o'clock, Kate handed me her house key. Standing a few feet away from her, I used my cell phone to call hers.

She answered her phone and smiled at me. "Who is it?" she said.

"Let's go," I said.

She left the office and took the elevator to the lobby. I wanted her to leave the building alone, so her admirer would continue to be careless about following her. If he saw me with her, I was sure he'd do a much better job of staying out of sight.

I expected him to follow her home and try to force his way into her apartment. But there was always the chance that he'd go after her in public. It wasn't a big chance, but it was a chance, so I wanted her to be on the phone, in contact with me, during every moment of her trip downtown.

I stood at the window and watched her as she crossed the street and went into the coffee shop. She was a brave young woman. She walked with a confident step.

"I'm in the Argo, big guy," she said.

"I can see that."

"I was thinking of ordering a scone. Do you think that's a good thing for a private detective's Gal Friday to nibble after a hard day's work?"

"I think that's a fine thing to nibble on."

"You don't think it's pretentious? You don't think I should order a donut instead?"

"No. A scone shows you're a classy broad."

We kept up a steady stream of nervous inanities as I left the building and got into my car, which was parked on 94th Street, within sight of the coffee shop. She was sitting in a booth near the plate glass window, so I could see her clearly.

A tall and heavyset man in a dark blue suit walked into the coffee shop.

"Thar she blows," she said.

"That's him?"

"That's our man."

The man sat down in a booth.

"Don't make eye contact," I said.

"No eye contact."

"Get the check," I said.

She caught the attention of a waitress and made a scribbling motion in the air.

I got out a pair of binoculars from my glove compartment and took a look at the man in the blue suit. He was very large. You could tell from his nose that he'd had a disputatious life.

Kate was looking intently at her scone, as if it was going to talk to her.

"What's he doing?" she said. "I'm scared to look at him."

"He's talking to the waiter."

"I wonder what he's saying."

"Speaking as a man who has a private detective's license, I've got a hunch that he's ordering something to eat."

"Yes, I *know* that. But *what* do you think he's going to eat, Singer? Do you think he's having dinner, or just a snack?"

She sounded a little giddy, or maybe a little hysterical.

"I'm not sure. Whatever he's having, I'm pretty sure it won't be a scone. He doesn't have enough class."

The counterman put a bowl and a breadbasket in front of Kate's admirer.

"I think he's having soup," I said.

"A soup dragon. What kind of soup is it?"

"Well, there are a few things we can eliminate. I don't think he's having matzoh ball soup, and we can probably also rule out borscht. Beyond that, I can't say."

"Think, Singer, think! It may be a clue!"

Kate's waitress put her check on the table, and Kate put some money down.

"You know what to do," I said.

She left the coffee shop and walked to the bus stop at Broadway and 94th. I could see the soup dragon turn and watch her through the window. When the bus arrived and Kate got on it, he paid for his soup and went outside. His got into a car that was double-parked a few doors down, and followed the bus.

I turned on my engine, drove up to 96th Street, turned east through Central Park, and went downtown on the FDR Drive. Kate lived all the way downtown, in the East Village. It would take her almost an hour to get there by bus. I wanted to arrive long before she did.

For the moment, Kate was safe, and although we hadn't broken the phone connection, we weren't bothering to talk. My phone was on the passenger seat; from time to time I could hear the bus stopping and starting, people getting on or off.

I parked in front of a fire hydrant on East 10th and Avenue A, near her apartment. Now came the tricky part. Would the soup dragon wait until Kate got to her building before making his move? Or would he catch up to her on the street after she got off the bus?

I thought he'd probably wait until she reached her building. He wouldn't want to accost her on the street: it would make no sense for him to trail her all the way down here only to assault her in a place where he could be interrupted or identified.

Of course, it's rarely a smart move to count on anybody's rationality, least of all that of a guy who makes his living by mauling people. Getting her alone in her lobby was the rational move for him. I was just hoping that he was smart enough to understand that.

This may sound odd, but I was reassured by the fact that he was wearing a suit. If he'd been some lunkhead in a muscle T, I would have considered him less predictable. His get-up increased the chances that he was a pro, and if he was a pro, he wouldn't do anything in plain sight.

I let myself into Kate's apartment with her key. Her cat came dancing up to greet me, pushing her neck against my ankles and purring loudly.

I got my phone out of the breast pocket of my jacket.

"You still there?"

"I'm still here," she said. "Calmly reading *Pride and Preju-dice.*"

"'It is a truth universally acknowledged'... Damn. I can't remember the rest."

"I'm disappointed in you," she said. "You might have to forfeit your membership in the Literary Gumshoes' Society."

"That would be a shame."

I took out my gun.

"Singer?"

"Yes?"

"Where does the word 'gumshoe' come from?"

I could feel her smiling over the phone.

"Do I look like Funk and Wagnall?" I said.

"You don't look like Funk. You might look a little like Wagnall, though."

I'd already checked my gun before I left the office, but I took a minute to check it again.

The gun was a family heirloom. My father bought it in the 1950s, when he worked for a labor union, organizing textile workers in the South. Then, as now, employers didn't take kindly to unionization; then, as now, they fought it with every tool they had—legal or illegal, it made no difference to them then, and makes no difference today. My father never had to use the gun, but it made him feel safer to have it as he traveled through a part of the country that often made him feel that—as a Jewish socialist labor organizer—he was in enemy territory. It was among his possessions when he died. I intended to sell it—I was still in graduate school, planning a dissertation on the poetry of Walt Whitman and William Blake, a pursuit for which a firearm did not seem necessary—but I never got around to it. It was still locked up in my desk drawer a year later, when I was working at the Ferruci agency and got promoted from researcher to investigator.

The gun was a well-made piece of machinery. If beauty in an object consists of the efficiency with which it performs its function, you could even say that it was beautiful. There was nothing about it that was wasteful, nothing that failed to contribute to its purpose. It was a masterpiece of design. My father had hated the thing. I hate guns too. But I didn't hate it, because it connected me to him, and because it enabled me to protect the lives of people I cared about. People like Kate.

"I'm in your apartment," I said.

"What do you think?"

"Very literary. That's no surprise. Very neat. That's not really a surprise either."

It was a tiny one-bedroom. There were bookcases along every wall. Paintings that I didn't recognize. They were interesting. Kate had taste.

"How's my kitty?"

"She seems in fine fettle. She might be a little hungry, though." The cat, still purring, was standing on its hind legs and resting its front paws beseechingly on my knee.

"There's a bag of Kibbles in the cabinet over the fridge."

I got out the bag and poured some of the dry brown things into her bowl.

"A full-service private detective," she said. "Shelters me from evildoers, feeds my cat."

"Where are you?" I said.

"Thirty-fourth and third." About ten minutes away.

"I'll be very impressed if you can remember my cat's name," she said.

"I never knew your cat's name."

"That's not true. I talk about her all the time. I definitely talked about her in August, when she had to get a kidney stone removed. And I know I told you her name."

"It's coming back to me now. It's either Rosa, after Rosa Luxemburg, or Emma, after Emma Goldman."

"That's completely wrong. You must be thinking of some political cat. My cat is named Emily, after Emily Dickinson."

As we were talking I was looking around her apartment. I felt certain that the main event would take place in the lobby—that's where he'd make his move on Kate, and that's where I'd make my move on him. But if everything went according to plan we'd end up here, and I wanted to get the lay of the land. I examined her front door, and pushed in the lock button so that the door wouldn't lock when it was closed.

"Do you have any masking tape, duct tape, anything like that?"

"In the desk in my bedroom," she said. "Bottom drawer."

"Good."

"What are you doing?" she said. "Duct taping my cat?"

"Not yet."

"Home improvement? You have a few minutes to spare and you're going to tape up a few of my ducts?"

"You know, Kate, it's a little known fact, but taping ducts is one of the few things that duct tape actually isn't good for."

"How do you know something like that?"

"When you're a private investigator, my dear, you have to know a lot of things about many different subjects."

It was actually something I'd learned the summer after high school, when I worked for a contractor in Boston for a couple of months.

"What is good for taping ducts?" she said.

"I know the answer to that," I said, "but if I told you—"

"You'd have to kill me. Yeah, I know."

While we were talking, I was finding the tape. I went back to the front door of her apartment, and, even though I'd already adjusted the lock button, I layered a few strips of tape on top of the lock. If the soup dragon somehow managed to make it into Kate's apartment with her, I wanted to make sure he couldn't lock me out.

I put my gun back into my hip holster—it was nicely concealed beneath my bookish tweed jacket—and went back down to the lobby.

Most of the buildings in the East Village were tenements, three- or four-story walk-ups. Kate's was a large pre-war apartment building; it must have been the soul of elegance, back in the day. You entered the building through a small unlocked entranceway or vestibule, which had a locked inner door that opened onto the lobby. The soup dragon, I was sure, would try to grab her just before she put her key in the lock, and force her up to her apartment.

"Elvis has left the building," Kate said. "In other words, I'm just getting off the bus. I'm at Third Avenue, heading your way."

I took up a position in a handy spot in the stairwell. Once they entered the lobby I could be on top of him in two steps.

There was one small light bulb in the stairwell. I unscrewed it. I could see the front door of the building, but no one entering the building was likely to see me.

"Block and a half to go," Kate said.

"Don't be too obvious about it, but get out your key. Have it in your hand so you don't have to look for it in the vestibule."

"OK," she said. "I'm getting it. Very inconspicuously. I've never thought of it as a vestibule, by the way."

"What do you think of it as?"

"I don't know. The place where the buzzers are."

I was nervous. I was worried about Kate. Even though I was staked out in a good spot, things can always go wrong.

Nervousness is good: it keeps you on your toes. Worry is not good: it makes you doubt yourself, makes you slow.

I held on to the nervousness and tried to dispel the worry. I could protect her. Nothing could stop me.

"Here I come," she said.

I saw her enter the vestibule, saw her put her key in the lock of the inner door. I was in the stairwell, in the dark. She knew I was nearby, but she didn't know exactly where.

She wasn't a tall woman, but the way she carried herself made it appear that she was. As she opened the lobby door, knowing that someone who wanted to harm her was only a short distance away, but nonetheless holding herself with her customary air of confidence, it struck me that she had a kind of nobility.

Kate was just removing her key from the door when he came

up behind her. He put one hand on her shoulder and said, "This will go easy for you if you keep your mouth shut."

"That's funny," I said, "because it will go easy for you if you talk." I could wisecrack like this because I already had my gun in his ear.

"Fuck," he said.

Which reassured me. When you have a gun pointed at somebody, it's very rare that he'll try to fight you or resist you in any way. But you can never be sure what people will do. So it was nice to see that he already knew the game was over.

He let go of Kate and the three of us headed upstairs.

"Fake out," Kate said to him, in a fifth-grade, schoolyard kind of voice. I thought she was going to stick her tongue out at him, but she didn't.

"Don't gloat," I said.

After we got into Kate's apartment I patted him down. He wasn't carrying anything except a car key. No gun, no blackjack, no wallet, no phone. This is the smart thing to do, for a guy like him in a situation like this—carry nothing that can be used to identify you—but people rarely do the smart thing.

I had him sit down in her rocking chair. Kate and I sat on the couch.

"What's your name?" I said to him.

"Mike," he said.

"Mike what?"

"My name's Mike. Let's leave it at that."

I had the feeling that I'd seen him before. But I couldn't remember where.

"What were you supposed to do here?"

"I was supposed to frighten the lady."

"And?"

"I was supposed to call you up. You're Singer, right? I was supposed to call you up, tell you I had her, give her the phone so she could blubber for a while, and tell you that I wasn't going to hurt her but the next time she wouldn't be so lucky. You know the routine."

"That was supposed to be it?"

"That was it."

I didn't believe him. I did know the routine, and I knew that the routine usually involves some rough stuff. Particularly when the routine includes grabbing a woman. Making the threat isn't enough; you have to get somebody bloody. But at this point the question was moot.

"You got one thing wrong, Mikey boy," Kate said.

"What's that?"

"You wouldn't have gotten me to blubber."

He shrugged.

"And who told you to pay my friend this visit?" I said.

"Who the hell do you think told me? You know as well as I do. Macy told me."

"Why? What's in this for Macy?"

"What's in this for Macy? Let's see. After I get home I'll fax you the mission statement." He shook his head at me gravely, as if he were disappointed in me for being so dumb. "I have no fucking idea what's in this for Macy. He told me what to do, he paid me, and I said I'd do it."

There was a notable absence of tension in the room. I still had my gun in my hand, but I had no fear that he was going to force me to use it.

It didn't surprise me, this absence of tension. He was a pro and I was a pro; I'd beaten him, and the game was over. For him to try anything now would make no sense; it would be like Arnold Palmer clubbing Jack Nicolaus on the head with a nine-iron after the last hole of the U.S. Open.

But at the same time, we both knew that if we went up against each other the next day or the next week, today's little jokes and ironies would mean nothing. If we found ourselves in a situation where one of us had to kill the other, neither of us would hesitate.

To put that more precisely: he wouldn't hesitate. And because I knew that he wouldn't hesitate, I would try not to hesitate either.

Kate got up, went to the refrigerator, and peered in.

"Can I get somebody something to drink?" she said. "Coffee,

tea? Or I've got peach juice, Diet Coke, and Vitamin Water, if you'd like something cold."

Mike shook his head at her and snorted. "Vitamin Water. That stuff is a complete rip-off. It's, like, tap water, and they add thirteen cents of vitamins and charge you two and a half bucks."

"First of all," Kate said, "I get it at Costco, so it comes out to about fifty cents a bottle. And second, it's not just water. It comes in a lot of different flavors."

I didn't interrupt them, just sat there while they went on like this, because I was trying to make space for my thoughts. A memory had been dislodged and was floating slowly upward. Finally it emerged.

"Mike my ass," I said. "You're Carl Packer."

"It's nice to be recognized," he said glumly. "How the hell do you know me?"

"You're the guy who set up that insurance scam out of Seattle two years ago. Home Health Solutions, right? I should be thanking you for that. It took me six months to untangle that whole thing. You paid my rent bills that year."

"My pleasure," he said.

Kate brought me some club soda and, just to be snarky, she brought Packer a glass of Vitamin Water.

"I have another question for you, Carl. Since when did you become a delivery boy?"

"What are you talking about?" Kate said to me. "I think I'm picking up on the idea that you two have some kind of rough respect for each other, but since I'm the person who Carl here was supposed to…evoke blubber from, I think I have a right to know what you're talking about."

"Evoke blubber from?" Carl said.

"Lay off, Carl," Kate said. "I'm in graduate school."

"What I was trying to say," I said, "was that Carl is a very proficient operator, and that for the last ten years or so he's been almost exclusively doing brainwork. So it's a surprise to see him doing a job this low-level and uncreative. Grab someone and make a threatening phone call. I would have thought that kind of thing would be beneath you, Carl."

"Nothing's beneath me if the price is right."

"And the price was right for this?"

He didn't bother answering.

"Who's behind Macy? Who's bankrolling this?"

Again he gave me that disappointed look. "I'll send you the prospectus," he said.

There was not much more to be learned here. I'd tossed out the question of who was bankrolling Macy, but I hadn't expected him to know. There would have been no reason for Macy to tell him.

"Now," I said to Kate, "we have to decide what to do with Carl."

"What's to decide?" Kate said. "We make him blubber and then we call his mom. She picks him up and tells him not to get mixed up in anything like this again."

Kate seemed to be intoxicated by the sheer adventure of it all.

"Carl," I said, "you understand that it's in your best interests if Detective Macy doesn't find out that things didn't go as planned tonight."

"Obviously," he said.

"So if I let you walk out the door, what Macy's going to hear from you is 'Mission accomplished.'"

"Mission accomplished. Isn't that what George Bush said about a month after we invaded Iraq? If he can say it, I can say it."

I turned to Kate. "It's your choice," I said. "We can call the cops and press charges, and Carl can spend a little time in jail. It might be satisfying, but in my opinion it isn't the smartest thing to do right now. Macy's going to know that this didn't work out, and he's going to try again. If Macy thinks that everything went well tonight, then it'll buy us some time, and hopefully we can wrap this thing up before he tries anything else."

"But if we press charges against Carl, can't we force Macy to tell us who's paying him?" Kate said.

"It's a good idea, but it wouldn't work. Macy would just deny everything—he'd say that he'd never even met Carl—and that would be that."

"And if we let him go?" Kate said. "I don't want to let him go if he's going to show up here tomorrow and try the same thing. I mean, no offense, Carl, it's been fun and all, but I don't want to see you ever again in my life."

I turned to Packer. "What do you have to say?"

"I've got a ticket on a flight to Paris tomorrow. I'm going on a vacation that I've been planning for a year. I'm spending two weeks in Paris, a week in Barcelona, and a week in Rome. Whoever Macy hires to come after you next, it won't be me."

I looked at Kate and she nodded.

"Have a good time," I said.

He didn't say anything, just headed for the door. But after he opened it, he stopped and turned back to us.

"A word to the wise," he said. "You shouldn't get too cocky because of what happened tonight. You're smart, but Macy's just as smart as you are. And he's a lot meaner. If I had to bet on this thing, I'm afraid I'd bet on Macy. So watch yourself."

After he left, Kate stood at the window so she could see him leave the building.

"You don't need to worry about Carl," I said. "He's not coming back."

"I believe you," she said. "I'm not sure why I believe you, but I believe you."

Even though it had all ended peacefully, the episode with Packer had left me tired. Holding a gun on someone is a mental strain, even if shots are never fired. At least it is for an admirer of Gandhi and Martin Luther King. It would have been nice to go home and relax. But I needed to make sure Kate didn't spend the rest of the night at home, brooding about how things might have turned out if Carl had been a little quicker or I'd been a little slower. Part of my job was making sure that Kate had a smooth landing.

I stood up. "Let me buy you a cup of coffee."

"I'd rather not go outside right now, if that's all right with you."

"I can understand that, Kate. But that's exactly why I think it would be a good idea to go outside. I don't want you to hole up in your apartment for the weekend, getting paranoid."

Kate assented to this, and we left the apartment and went to a diner on St. Mark's Place.

"I've never known you to have a meal in a real restaurant," she said. "I guess you're a diner boy."

"I know. I wish I had more class. Did you hope I would take you to the Ritz?" I said. I wasn't even sure the Ritz existed anymore.

"No. I like your diner thing. It's old-fashioned. You're old-fashioned. It's one of the things I like about you."

It was true that I did have a sense of loyalty to the old-time diners of Manhattan. The New York I knew was disappearing, and I didn't want to help speed its demise, so I usually ate at little mom-and-pop diners that had been around for a decade or two.

I ordered a cup of coffee. Kate had a cup of herbal tea and a bowl of peach cobbler.

She was smiling at me oddly from the other side of the booth.

"What?"

"I think I'm starting to figure you out, Singer."

"What does that mean?"

"Do you remember the first time we met? When I came in to interview for the job? I told you I was in a graduate writing program and you told me that you once wanted to be a poet, and that you eventually gave it up."

"Sure. I remember that."

"And then I said that I sometimes thought I should stop writing, because I'm not sure I'm good enough. And you said the important thing wasn't how good you are, but how much you need to do it. You said that a writer is somebody who *needs* to write, and that the reason you stopped writing poetry was that you found out that you didn't need to."

"OK. I said all that."

"The things you said that day meant a lot to me. I remember you said that you had a few classmates who'd gone on to become artists of one kind or another, and you said they weren't actually the most talented people in the class. You said the thing that made them stand out over the long term was how much they loved doing it. You said that they were in love with making art, and part of what that meant was that they weren't just in love with it when it went well, they were in love with it when it was going badly. You said that they were even in love with the difficulties of art."

"I must have been in a talkative mood that day."

"You were. Maybe you were trying to impress me because you thought I was so pretty, and you wanted to make sure I'd end up taking the job."

"That might have had something to do with it."

"I remember you said that you found out that a person can't choose to be an artist. You said that art either chooses you or it doesn't, and that poetry just didn't choose you."

"It's true. That's how it felt to me. It was like going to a dance and hoping to get picked. Poetry didn't ask me to dance."

"And then you went to graduate school in literature, right?"

"Yeah. For a year. I thought if I wasn't going to write poetry, the next best thing would be to teach it."

"And what happened?"

"I got a job as a P.I. At first I thought I was doing it just to pay my way through grad school, but I found out that I loved it."

"I remember you said that you had this moment that was like a light bulb going on over your head."

"I did."

"What was it? I always meant to ask."

"It was about three or four weeks after I got out from behind the research desk. I was looking for this missing kid. Teenager. I eventually tracked him down in Canada, but that's another story. His name was Billy Blake. I was spending every waking hour thinking about him, trying to figure out why he'd disappeared and where he'd disappeared to. I wasn't only thinking about it at work, I'd be thinking about it at home, I'd be thinking about it when I was in the classroom. And it struck me one day that I felt much more committed, much more alive, when I was trying to figure out what was going on with Billy Blake, than when I was thinking about William Blake—the poet I was supposed to be writing my thesis about. That was the moment when I realized I wanted to leave grad school. When I realized I was already doing what I wanted to be doing."

"And have you ever regretted it? Have you ever regretted not becoming an English professor?

"Never. When I'm doing my job—this job—I have a deep down feeling that this is what I was meant to do."

"When you were growing up, did you ever think you might end up being a detective?"

"Nope. I always thought I was going to be some sort of art-ist. Poet, novelist, something like that. I certainly wasn't planning on being any kind of a cop, private or otherwise. That wasn't on the career path for a sensitive Jewish kid from New Jersey."

Kate was smiling triumphantly.

"What?" I said.

"Just like I told you: I figured you out. You thought that art didn't choose you, but you were wrong. Art did choose you. It just wasn't the art you thought it was going to be."

"I'm not following you."

"Everything about your background says that you shouldn't be a detective. Everything in your background said that you were sup-posed to end up a poet, like you wanted to be, or a teacher. You were supposed to end up teaching Late Romantic poetry at Columbia and wearing tweed jackets with little patches on the elbows. You were sup-posed to be a professor whose awkward shyness made him endearing to his students. But instead you were chosen, by an art form. Like you said, you can't choose to be an artist—art either chooses you or it doesn't. The art of poetry didn't choose you. But what did choose you was the art of being a detective. The art of being a detective asked you to dance. The art of saving people's lives. And because you're a true artist, you've built your life around it. I don't know anything about your personal life, really, but my guess is that you've sacrificed a lot in order to remain true to your art."

I wasn't used to this kind of attention—wasn't used to having the magnifying glass trained on *me*. I was about to ward it all off with a joke. But I decided not to.

"That's a nice way to think of it," I said. "That's a nice thing to say. Thank you."

"Thank *you*," she said.

"For what?"

"For saving me from Mikey. Mikey Carl."

"I don't know if you can thank me for saving you from him. Technically."

"Why is that?"

"Because if you hadn't gotten mixed up with me, he wouldn't have been coming after you in the first place."

"Well," she said, "that's true."

# Chapter eighteen

As I drove uptown, I checked the voice mail at my office. I had three messages. The first was from Mrs. Carpenter.

"Hi. It's me. I mean, it's Natalie Carpenter. I don't know why I think you should know what I'm talking about when I say 'it's me.' I'm not 'me' to you, am I? You hardly know me." There was a long pause. Then she said, "I wonder if your voice mail has an 'erase this message and start again' option."

It didn't. That was the end of the message.

The second message was also from Mrs. Carpenter.

"Well, it's me again. This time I *can* say it's me, not because I've become an 'it's me' to you in the last ten minutes, but because I made the mistake of saying 'it's me' ten minutes ago. So you know who 'me' is. I'll give you a second to take all that in while I freshen my drink." I heard ice dropping into a glass, liquid being poured. "I was calling because I wanted to know how things were going. And I was calling because you said that I should never hesitate to call you, even if I don't have a specific reason. At least I think you said that. Maybe I just wanted you to say that."

There was a long pause while she thought about this, and then my voice mail cut her off.

And the third message was from…Mrs. Carpenter. "I'm just calling to say you should ignore my calls. I'm fine. I'm getting ready for bed, and I'm going to have a nice sleep, and in the morning things will feel better. I'm sure. Things feel better in the morning."

She'd left this message only about a minute ago. I called her from my car.

"It's very nice of you to call," she said when she answered. "But you didn't have to. You got that message where I told you you didn't have to call? I think it was the fifteenth message I left you."

"I got that one, yes."

"So you know you didn't have to call me."

"I know that. But I wanted to call you anyway."

"Why?"

"I wanted to see how you are."

There was a silence on the other end of the line.

"Mrs. Carpenter?"

I heard her taking another drink. "You're a good man, Mr. Singer."

People were blowing their horns at each other not too far away from me.

"Are you in your car?" she said.

"Yes."

"Would it be out of line to ask if you would mind coming over?"

"No. Not at all. I'd be happy to."

I don't know if I was actually happy to, but I didn't mind. Trying to help your clients keep it together is part of the job.

I got to her place about ten minutes later. When she opened the door, I was dismayed to find that she was in a bathrobe. It's not that she was dressed for seduction. She wasn't. She wasn't in a nightgown; she wasn't in a negligee. Her bathrobe was a thick pink terrycloth thing, and she had a towel wrapped around her hair. Using the skills that I had honed over more than a decade, I deduced that she had just taken a shower.

The reason I was dismayed was that even though she wasn't dressed for seduction, even though she was distraught and probably drunk, she was an arresting woman, and it would be all too easy to do something dumb. My job was to help her, not to get involved with her in any other way. Getting involved with a client is never a good idea, and getting involved with a client who is bereft and lonely is worse. It's not merely careless, it's unethical.

"You got here faster than I thought," she said. "I wanted to make myself presentable. Please give me a minute. Make yourself at home. You can help yourself to anything in the liquor cabinet. And there's a little refrigerator behind the bar."

While she was gone I looked at the photographs on the wall. All of them were of her husband receiving awards. She appeared in only one of them. He was in the center of it, shaking Bill Clinton's hand; she was standing way off to the side.

She reemerged from the bedroom wearing a sweater and dark pants. Better. I could think now.

"It's very good of you to come," she said. "You must be sick of me. You must want to get to the bottom of all this as quick as you can, just so you can get me out of your life."

"That's not the way I feel, Mrs. Carpenter."

"You didn't make yourself a drink. What can I get you? Beer? Wine? Something stronger?"

"Nothing. Thank you."

"That's right. You don't drink on the job. But on the other hand, it's ten o'clock at night. Are you still on the job?"

"Still on the job."

She looked at me as though she was making an assessment.

"I think you're probably always on the job."

I didn't say anything to that.

"Can I get you something else? A Shirley Temple? Is that the private detectives' drink of choice these days?"

"I'll have a club soda, please, if you've got it."

She went to the kitchen. It said a lot about her that she didn't walk like a drunk. She walked gracefully.

She returned with a club soda for me and some unidentifiable brown drink for herself.

"I feel like the world has been ripped away from me," she said. "Like there's been an earthquake, and I was standing on one side of the fault, and everything else in my life was on the other. Everything in my life is gone. I can't get back there. But I just don't know how to start over."

"The other day you told me that you used to think you'd be a schoolteacher someday."

"That's right. I always knew that I wasn't going to have children of my own. I always knew I was too selfish. Too selfish to give my entire life over to a child the way you have to do to be a good mother. But I wanted to be around children, and I wanted to be of use. I thought that would be a wonderful thing to do."

"A friend of mine is an administrator at a private school in Brooklyn," I said. "Saint Ann's. It's a pretty nice school."

"I know Saint Ann's. Some of our friends' kids go there."

"I could find out if they have any openings."

"Openings for someone with a twenty-year-old degree in education, who's never stood in front of a classroom in her life?"

"They're a pretty unorthodox place. They don't care that much about credentials. They care about things like intelligence and commitment."

"Do you think I'm strong enough? I've led a very pampered life for a long time, Mr. Singer. Can you see me getting up at seven and working all day and then coming home and preparing for the next day's class?"

"I can see you doing anything you want to do."

"You really believe I can change myself that much?"

"I do."

She looked down into her drink.

"I think I know another thing you believe."

"What's that?"

"I think you believe my husband was murdered."

"Why do you say that?"

"There's something different about you tonight. When I've seen you before, I thought you were being kind to me. I wanted you to look into my husband's death, and you were being nice by taking me seriously. You're being kind to me tonight, too, but there's something else now. You look like someone who has the scent of blood and isn't going to stop until he finds out where it leads. Is that true?"

"I haven't really discovered anything about your husband's death yet. But I won't say you're wrong."

"Can you tell me anything more about that?"

"I'm sorry. Not yet."

"Why not?"

"I never like to tell my clients anything until I know what I'm talking about."

If I thought she could help me, I would have told her something about what I'd learned. But I already knew that she didn't have any suspicions about Macy—she thought he was just an unsympathetic cop, not a cop with an interest in covering up the truth about her husband's death. And I wasn't about to ask her if she knew anybody with a red sports car. I needed to have something more definite than that.

We were silent for a long time. Finally I stood up to go.

"I'll be in touch with you tomorrow," I said.

She walked me to the door. "Thank you."

"For what?"

"For your kindness. And for your professionalism."

"My professionalism."

"It's an unusual situation. You're in my home. It's late. I'm lonely. I'm needy. I can feel your self-restraint. And I'm grateful for it."

"I'll call you tomorrow, Mrs. Carpenter."

"Thank you."

It took me about forty-five minutes to get home. I lived in Jersey, in the house that Claire and I had bought shortly after Wini was born. Selling the place and moving into the city had been near the top of my to-do list ever since Claire and I had split up. But I hadn't gotten around to doing it. After all, it had only been two years.

# Chapter nineteen

When I got home the phone was ringing.

The caller didn't bother to introduce himself. It was Macy.

"I hope that cute little secretary of yours isn't too much the worse for wear."

Clearly Packer had reported back to him already and had told him that everything went fine.

"You shouldn't look at her as damaged goods, Singer," he continued. "I'm sure she'll be as good as new after a little bit of cosmetic surgery."

"What do you want?"

"All I want is for you to go back to your normal life. You make a nice little living with those workmen's comp cases, don't you? It doesn't make any sense to get in over your head. You're not used to playing with the big boys, and you're going to get hurt."

I didn't say anything. I wanted to gloat: I wanted to let him know that his plans hadn't quite worked out. But that, of course, would not have been wise.

"That's it, Singer," he said. "Think about it. Maybe take some time off so you can think about it in a nice, calm way. Maybe take some time off and visit your wife. You're not even officially divorced yet, are you? Maybe you can patch things up. Hang out a little bit with those two cute kids of yours."

"Fuck you," I said, and hung up.

## Chapter twenty

Calling Claire was the last thing I wanted to do. But I called her.

She was living in California now, so at least she wouldn't be asleep.

"Nathaniel," she said, before I said a word. Caller ID.

"Did Jack get the books?"

"Yes, Nathaniel. Jack got the books."

"Did they arrive on his birthday?"

"They arrived on his birthday."

"So what's the problem?"

"If you have to ask, Nathaniel," she said, "you'll never know."

"Indulge me."

"The problem is that although it was nice for Jack to get books on his birthday, it would have been even nicer if he had gotten a phone call from his father on his birthday."

*I was busy looking into the probably accidental death of someone I never knew.*

That line wouldn't have gone over too well.

It probably wouldn't have gone over too well, either, if I had reminded her that she was the one who had moved across the country after we separated, and I was the one who had wanted us to continue living in the same town so I could play a role in Wini's and Jack's lives.

This wasn't an argument that we needed to rehash again.

When Claire and I met, I was still in graduate school. She was amused, maybe charmed, that I was moonlighting as a detective, and when I left graduate school to become a detective full-time, she supported the decision. She could see that I loved what I was doing.

It was only after we had kids that she began to grow uncomfortable with what I did. By that time I had moved out from the desk and become a field operative, and I'd gotten hurt once or twice. I hadn't gotten seriously hurt, but that was only because I was lucky.

Everything changed for good when somebody shot up the car. It was after I'd spent half a year gathering evidence to put a loan sharking ring away. One day after work one of the leg-breakers trailed me over the George Washington Bridge and when I stopped at Carvel's to get a cake for Wini's birthday, he put a few holes in the windshield. If he'd been more patient, it would have been me he was filling with holes, but because of his lack of impulse control I was able to walk away unharmed. Claire took it for granted that I'd change jobs after that—at the very least she thought I'd go back behind the desk and confine myself to research, so none of the future bad guys would even know my name. But it never occurred to me to change jobs. My thought was that I'd be more careful next time—I shouldn't have let the bastard trail me—and that we'd get an unlisted phone number. At first Claire thought I was joking, and then she thought I was out of my mind. She left me less than two months later.

"I need to tell you something. Something that isn't going to make you happy."

"What is that, Nathaniel?" She used my name a lot when she was angry. And she stopped using contractions.

"There's been some trouble here, and I think it would be a good idea for you and the kids to visit your mom for a while."

"You think we should visit my mom." This was a habit that I'd first noticed when things started to go bad with us: when I said things that displeased her, she would repeat them, slowly. "And how long do you think this visit should last?"

"Ten days. Maybe two weeks. I'm pretty sure I should have everything cleared up by then." Although I wasn't sure how.

"And if you don't?"

"Don't worry. I will."

"You know, Nathaniel, I was thinking about you the other night. After it passed midnight on Jack's birthday and you hadn't called. And I realized something."

"What was that?"

"I used to think that I loved you but I hated your life. It's taken me a long time to understand that you *are* your life. You chose this life. It didn't choose you. And you choose it over and over again, every day."

"I know that."

"I used to think I knew the real you," she said. "I used to think the real you was the man who made me so happy, the wonderful father that you sometimes were. The man who knew what the children needed before they knew it themselves. The man who seemed to be able to look at them and see what they were thinking. The man who used to make our children laugh until they were almost crying. I thought that was the real you. I know that those parts of you *were* real. But it took me so long to realize that they weren't your core."

"We can take this up later, Claire. Can you just tell me that you and the kids will get away for a little while?"

"Yes, Nathaniel."

"Thank you. I'll call you soon."

"Nathaniel?"

"Yes?"

"Take care of yourself, OK?"

"I'll try," I said.

# Chapter twenty-one

It would have been reasonable to think that my work was over for the night. I was in a heavy sleep when the phone rang.

"Mr. Singer?" A woman's voice, whispering. "Thank God you're in."

"Who is this?"

"It's Amy. Amy Roth."

It was only about ten at night, although it felt like three in the morning.

"I got back from my sister's last night. The things I told you about—the evidence about Reverend Underwood. I'm not sure I told you where I was keeping them. I was keeping them at my sister's."

"So you have the evidence with you now?"

"Yes. I do. But I think the Reverend Underwood knows."

"What do you think he knows?"

"I think he knows that I met with you the other day. I think he knows I have information that could hurt him. I think he knows I'm going to give it to you."

"What makes you think he knows all this, Amy?"

"When I went into work today, he was looking at me very strangely. He was looking at me very strangely all day."

I wasn't sure what this might mean. It was possible that someone had seen us together in Tarrytown, someone who'd reported back to Underwood. It was much more likely that she was just nervous, and had brought her nervousness into work that day. If Underwood really had looked at her strangely, it was probably just because she'd been acting strange.

"Why don't you just go to sleep, Amy, and I'll be up there first thing in the morning. Before you go to work. And we can sort everything out then. If this material is as damning as you say it is, you might not ever have to look at Reverend Underwood again."

"I don't know if it can wait until tomorrow morning. I can't explain why, Mr. Singer, but I don't have a good feeling right now."

"Did you see anyone following you home?"

"I didn't see anyone. But before I left I saw Reverend Underwood talking to Mr. Teller, and I had this feeling that they were talking about me."

Teller. The guy I thought of as Charlie Chaplin. I didn't think she was in danger, but I wasn't sure.

I got out of bed and started looking for my clothes.

"OK, Amy. Just sit tight. I'm going to come up and get you."

"Thank God," she said.

"Are your doors locked?"

"Yes. I always lock them when I get home."

"Well, double-check. Make sure your windows are locked too. If you hear anything suspicious, call 911 right away. And then call me on my cell."

"Thank you."

"And you should probably hide the stuff about Underwood." I had put on my pants and taken out my gun.

"I don't have it with me."

"Where is it?" I was on my way out the door.

"I put it in my desk in the office. It's safe. I keep the desk drawer locked."

"All right. Just sit tight. You're going to be fine."

It took me a little more than half an hour to make it to Tarrytown at eighty miles per hour.

When I got close to her place I called her. I got her machine. I called her again. I got her machine again.

When I rang her doorbell, she didn't respond.

The outer door of her two-family house was locked, but it wasn't hard to jimmy.

I knocked at the door of her apartment. No response.

The lock on her apartment door took a while. As I worked on it, I heard nothing coming from inside.

I know cops who claim to be able to read silences. They say that when they stand in front of a locked door, they can tell whether the silence on the other side is the silence of an empty apartment or the silence of an apartment in which someone is dead. I've never been able to read silences like that, but I had a bad feeling as I worked on the door.

I finally got it open. The apartment was dark. I turned the light on. There was no one in the living room. The room had obviously been ransacked, quickly and recklessly, by someone who was looking for something in particular. The drawers and the closet door were thrown open and things were tossed all over the floor. All of the books had been swept off the room's only bookshelf.

I went into the bedroom. Amy Roth was lying on the floor. Her eyes were open. Her head was at a right angle to her neck.

For no real reason, I felt for a pulse. I knew I wouldn't find one. Her body was still warm.

I knew where I had to go next, and I wanted to get there quickly. But I took a moment to look around the room. There were signs of a struggle, and a search, with things strewn all over the floor. But you could see that the person who had lived here had been orderly, careful, and sentimental. There were a few paintings on the walls: wide-eyed puppies, mischievous kittens. There were stuffed animals on the bed, and on the top of the dresser drawer was a figurine of Mickey Mouse. Mickey had been designed to hold a photograph: he had his arms outstretched and he had a slot in each hand. The photograph that had been fitted into the slot showed Amy and a small girl, holding hands in front of the "Small World" exhibit at Disneyland. There were words printed on Mickey's base: "I love my _____ this much." In the blank space a childish hand had written carefully "Auntie Amy." I love my Auntie Amy this much.

This must have been the niece that Amy had mentioned, when she said that she had to expose Underwood's crimes, whatever the risks, because she'd always told her niece how important it was to stand up for your beliefs.

If not for me, I thought, she would still be alive. She might have had many more decades, decades in which to go to Disneyland with her niece. Maybe she would have gotten married. Maybe she would have had children. By poking around in her life, asking questions, asking her to help me, I had led her toward her death.

I drove toward the headquarters of the Party of God. When I got there I parked on the street and took my handy tool kit with me. Also my gun.

The security booth was empty. There was only one vehicle in the parking lot. Underwood's Hummer.

It was after midnight, but the building was unlocked. Underwood had driven straight here after killing Amy, and either because of his haste or because he was rattled, he hadn't bothered to lock the front door behind him.

I could see light seeping from under the door of an office at the far end of the dimly lit corridor. It was Amy's office.

Amy's office was connected to Frye's, I remembered. They had separate entrances. I took out my lock-picking tools and worked on Frye's door as quietly as I could. It took me a few minutes, but finally I got it open.

There was little danger of Underwood hearing me. He was making a fair amount of noise himself, grunting like an animal. At one point I heard him say, "Fuck this shit! Goddammit!" Very un-reverend-like.

From what I remembered of the layout of Amy's office, I knew that whether he was looking for something in Amy's computer or desk or filing cabinets, he wouldn't be facing the door that connected the office to Frye's. I open it very slightly, just a crack.

The Reverend Underwood was attempting to open one of Amy's desk drawers. He was going at it with great determination but little skill. He had a knife in his hand, which he was trying to use crowbar-fashion to pry the drawer open.

Finally it worked. Something popped, the drawer slid open, and Underwood began rummaging through the files.

"Fuck," he said. "Fuck, fuck, fuck, fuck, fuck."

I heard the faint sound of footsteps approaching down the long carpeted hall.

"Jonathan, what on earth is this all about?"

It was Frye. I couldn't see him yet. He was standing in the doorway of Amy's office.

"Isn't it obvious, Arthur?" Underwood said.

"Nothing about this is obvious, Jonathan. It isn't obvious why you called me at *midnight* to tell me you had something you needed to discuss with me. It isn't obvious why you couldn't talk about it over the phone. And it isn't obvious why you are now sitting at my secretary's desk, looking as if you've just been through a street fight. Now please tell me what on earth is going on."

"What's going on, Arthur, is that I had a talk with your secretary earlier this evening, and now I'm going through her files."

"Why? Why are you looking through Amy's files?"

"Do we really need to play dumb? Even at this late date?"

"I really don't know what you're talking about. If you're going to insist on acting both mysterious and...*unhinged*, then I think I might as well just go back home."

"You must think I'm blind. You had such a convenient arrangement. You had Little Miss Muffet here at your beck and call. Your worshiper, your playmate, and your spy. I know you were sleeping with her, and I know you had her spying on me. Don't look so shocked. You don't think I believed you were employing your little friend because of her secretarial abilities, do you? She was a sweet girl, but she had the brain of a pigeon."

"What do you mean 'was'?"

"We're catching on now, aren't we Arthur? Your dear Miss Roth is no longer with us. With her usual punctuality, she arrived a little bit early for her appointment with her maker."

"What on earth are you talking about?"

"I'll tell you what I'm talking about. Your sweet little lapdog isn't going to be spying on me anymore. In a day or two, the police are going to find her body. And they're going to find her body next to the body of her lover, who broke her neck and then shot himself in the head."

"Have you taken leave of your senses?"

"I don't think so, Arthur. I don't think so."

Underwood picked up a briefcase and put it on Amy's desk. He opened it, placed the files carefully inside, and produced a revolver.

"You've tried your best to ruin everything the Party of God has stood for," Underwood said. "I've watched you undermining everything for years—our methods and our values. Did you really think I was just going to sit here and take it forever?"

I could see that Underwood was just getting started. He was going to shoot Frye eventually, but first he was going to try to lecture him to death. I knew I had a minute to think.

Sometimes it's better, though, *not* to have time to think. When you have a minute, some very ugly thoughts can pass through your mind.

I remembered what Clarence Lincoln had told me about the Party of God. That Underwood was the safer leader, because most Americans would be able to see that he was a buffoon: a moral and political simpleton, a fanatic, a thug. Frye was more dangerous because he was more effective. Under Underwood, the Party of God would become a laughing stock; under Frye, its influence would grow.

What if I were to wait? What if I waited until Underwood killed Frye? I could then storm in and disarm him and have the satisfaction not only of bringing a murderer to justice but of destroying the future of a hate-mongering organization. And no one on earth would know what I had done. No one on earth, not even Underwood, would know that I could have saved Frye if I'd chosen to. No one on earth would know that my hands were stained with Frye's blood.

"Put down the gun, Underwood, or I'll blow your head off." I said this quietly, unemphatically, as I opened the door.

Whether or not my thought had been a good one, I couldn't do it. I couldn't stand there and let Underwood kill Frye. I spoke. "Put the gun on the floor, very slowly, and then stand back up."

Underwood looked at me, and for a moment I thought he was going to turn toward me and fire. But then he realized that I could kill him before he so much as moved his arm. He knelt and put his gun on the floor.

The scent of urine filled the room.

"Don't worry," I said to Frye. "That's a perfectly normal response."

I kicked Underwood's gun away and told him to lie on the floor.

Frye had tears in his eyes. "The will of the Lord was working through you tonight, Mr. Singer. Of that I'm sure."

"If the will of the Lord had been working through me, he would have gotten me up here a little faster. Before your co-religionist here killed Amy Roth."

I called the police. Frye left the room to clean himself up. He actually asked my permission—that's how shaken he was. While he was gone I took the files from Underwood's briefcase, removed the papers from the file folders, and put the papers in my jacket.

The cops who showed up were still in their twenties; they looked like they were pretending to be cops for a high-school play. When they got Underwood up off the floor, he was smirking, but he stopped when he realized that he didn't recognize either of them.

"Who are you?" he said. "I don't know you."

"State police," one of them said. "You were expecting some-body else?"

I had remembered Amy telling me that the local police were

all in Underwood's pocket, and I'd thought it prudent to call the state police instead.

I told them that I'd apprehended Underwood in the act of attempting to murder Frye. Frye corroborated this.

"There's a dead woman across town," I said. I gave them Amy Roth's address. "I have a feeling that you'll find the Reverend's prints all over her throat."

"And who are you?" the cop said.

I spent another two hours there, answering the same questions over and over, and finally had to put in a call to Keller. But at last they told me I was free to go.

When I reached my car, I looked through Amy's files on Underwood. It was an impressive collection. If by some miracle he succeeded in beating the rap for her murder, the information she'd compiled about him would be enough to put him behind bars for a long time. He'd embezzled money from the Party of God; he'd dug up some dirt on one of the Party's chief financial backers and was extracting ten thousand dollars of hush money once a month; he had paid a detective to come up with something he could use to blackmail Frye. Evidently the detective hadn't come up with anything yet.

For my purposes, the most important thing about the files was what *wasn't* there: There was nothing about Dr. Carpenter, nothing to indicate that Underwood might have had a role in killing him. Of course I hadn't expected to find a smoking gun—I knew there wouldn't be cancelled checks that Underwood had written out to a hit man—but when you go through a person's financial records, seeing what he's done, you also get a smell for what he hasn't done, what he wouldn't do. Underwood had been a horrible man for a long time, and now he had become a killer, but I didn't think he'd ever killed anyone before, and I didn't think he'd ever paid to have anyone killed.

My dealings with the Party of God were over. It was still possible that the death threats had been written by someone from the organization, or someone influenced by it, but I'd have to fingerprint every zealot in the tri-state area to find out.

This kind of thing happens all the time in my profession. You can spend days or weeks or months patiently following a thread to see where it leads you, only to find that it's led you down a dead end. Sometimes I think the main characteristic a detective needs to hone is patience. You need the patience to understand that ending up at dead ends is an unavoidable part of the process, the patience to understand that you have to start over the next day by picking up another thread, which might be the one that leads you to the heart of the matter, or might just lead you down another dead end.

So I didn't regret the time I'd spent pursuing a lead that hadn't gone anywhere. But I was still reeling from the fact that by poking around in all this, I'd set off a chain of events that had led to Amy Roth's death.

# Chapter twenty-two

The next morning I woke up early and went for a long run around the Oradell Reservoir. Then I drove to White Plains for a meeting with my contact at one of the insurance agencies I freelance for. It was a meeting I could have postponed, but I wanted to take a day off from the Carpenter case.

I knew what the next steps had to be. I had to start over again, interviewing more people who knew him, finding out more about what he was like, whether he had any enemies and who they might be. And of course I had to make sure that Kate followed up on tracing the partial license plate number that I'd given her.

I knew what the next steps had to be, but I didn't want to take them right away. I felt miserable about Amy Roth's death, and I needed to take a day doing things that I could accomplish automatically, without thinking.

When I got to my office the next morning, Kate was already there, looking vibrant and well rested. She didn't look like someone who'd had a goon come after her two nights before.

I'd come up with two containers of coffee, and put one in front of her.

She looked up and smiled brightly.

"Bingo," she said.

"Bingo?"

"I found the car."

"Tell me," I said.

"There's a red Mazda convertible, license KNG 989, owned by a Mr. and Mrs. Benjamin Lipton of Larchmont."

"How do you know it's red?"

"I took a trip up to Larchmont yesterday."

"You're kidding! Just to check out the car?"

She was beaming, proud of herself.

"That's fantastic, Kate. Thank you."

"Am I the best or am I the best?" she said.

She's a top-notch assistant, but she's not very modest.

## Chapter twenty-three

I was ringing the doorbell of the Liptons' house in Larchmont.

The red Mazda convertible was in the driveway. But no one was answering. I went back to my car, where I had a thermos full of coffee and my book on forgery. I waited.

Nothing happened for the first hour. Or the second.

After I had been there two and a half hours, a postman came down the block pushing his mail cart. He was a short, stocky man with a moustache. He walked past the Lipton house without breaking stride.

I caught up with him and walked with him for a couple of steps.

"Can you tell me where the Liptons are?"

"How should I know?"

"Because you deliver their mail?"

He stopped walking. "And if I know, why should I tell you?"

I took out my wallet and flipped it open so he could see my investigator's license.

"They may have information that's relevant to a case I'm working on," I said.

I was accompanying him up the long walkway of the next house. He reached into his bag and pulled out a bundle of mail held together with rubber bands.

"Now my hunch," he said, "speaking strictly as an amateur, is that those things must be a little bit cool and a little bit frustrating."

"What things?"

"Detective licenses."

"How's that?"

"I bet you find that people are divided into two groups. I bet about half the people you show it to are impressed by it, and immediately tell you what you want to know. And I bet the other half say something like, 'So you're a private detective. Who the hell cares? I don't have to talk to you. You're not a real cop.'"

He was smirking, taking a lot of pleasure in being a wise guy.

"That's about right," I said. "And which group would you yourself happen to belong to?"

"I'm in a category all by myself," he said. He put the first-class mail in the box, sorted through one of the pouches on his cart, removed a copy of *Gourmet* magazine, and put that in the box as well.

"And what category would that be?" I said.

"I'm someone who, when they see something like that, just likes to bust the person's balls."

"It sounds to me like that puts you in the second category, though. The people who tell me that they don't have to talk to me."

"Maybe. But most people in that category just won't talk to you, period. I lead you on a little. I make you work a little. I don't talk to you, with style."

There were days on which, if I had encountered this man, I would have bantered with him for five or ten minutes, to find out if, after busting my chops for a while, he would tell me what I wanted to know. And there were days on which I would have threatened him. He looked like someone who would scare easily, and I was pretty sure that if I just planted myself in front of him and sort of... loomed, it wouldn't take more than a jiffy for him to tell me where the Liptons were.

But I didn't feel like doing any of those things today. I didn't have the patience to banter with him, and Amy Roth's death had left me feeling ill. I could find out what I wanted to know through violence, or through the threat of violence, but I didn't want to do that today. Normally I looked upon violence and the threat of violence as tools, to be employed with intelligence and care, but at that moment, on a peaceful little street in the peaceful little suburban enclave of Larchmont, I was yearning for a world in which violence, even the idea of violence, did not exist.

Without saying another word to him, I started back to my car.

"Hey. Where are you going?"

I just kept walking.

"What's this? This is how you investigate? Somebody tells you they don't want to talk to you and you just walk away? You just give up?"

He was at my side now. He had actually trotted after me, leaving his little pushcart on the sidewalk.

"If you want to talk to me, talk to me," I said. "If you don't, don't. I can find out what I need to know from someone else. I really don't have time to keep you company while you get your jollies by being a wise guy."

"You're no fun at all," he said.

"Sorry."

I got into my car.

"Well, Mr. Lipton moved out about a year ago. Sad. They always seemed like a nice couple. When he first moved out, his mail was getting forwarded to Manhattan. I don't know if he's still there. Mrs. Lipton's in Westport. That's where her mail's been going, at least. I don't remember the exact address. But I remember it's Westport."

"How long has she been gone?"

143

"About a week, ten days."

"When's she coming back?"

"I don't know. The forwarding order didn't have an end date."

"Thanks."

I got into my car and put the key in the ignition. He was standing at the window.

"Aren't you going to—"

I didn't hear the rest of what he said. I was already driving away.

## Chapter twenty-four

I knew only one or two people in the society world. One of them was a woman I considered a friend. Her name was Beth Palmer. I called her and asked if she knew who the Liptons were. She knew more than that. She'd been friendly with the Liptons for years. I asked if she was free for dinner. She was.

We met at Café Loup on West 13th Street. With her glowing skin and calm brown eyes, Beth looked as splendid as ever. I had known her in graduate school, a long time ago, and I might have been half in love with her, but it was hard to remember. Our lives had gone such different ways.

She was married now, with two kids. When Claire and I were still together, we sometimes used to get together with Beth and Harry. I hadn't seen much of them since we had split up, but I'd reached out to Beth a few times when I needed inside information about the world of the rich and the superrich.

"I love it when you call me," she said. "I feel so…useful."

"You don't feel useful the rest of the time?" Beth was a lawyer and sat on the board of several liberal foundations.

"I do, but in a different way. When I'm feeling useful to you, it's exciting. I always feel like you're just about to say, 'Palmer! The game's afoot!' and pull me into some dangerous adventure."

"I'll have to do that sometime," I said.

"It would be nice if you did."

"So what can you tell me about the Liptons?" I asked.

"I've known Joanna since college. I used to know her quite well. We never spent much time together one on one, but we had a lot of mutual friends. These days I only see her once or twice a year, at dinner parties or charity events. But I'm always very happy to meet up with her. She's so real. With most of the people you meet at these things, when they tell you a story, no matter what the subject of the story is, no matter the ostensible point, what they're really doing is boasting about how wealthy they are. Joanna isn't like that. She values people because of what they do, not because of what they're worth. She's a remarkable woman. I've really always thought of her as a kind of hero."

"A hero? Why?"

"She got away from that father of hers, for one thing."

"What was wrong with her father?"

"Pretty much everything. Don't you know who her father is?"

I didn't.

"Her father is Sandy Heller," she said.

"*The* Sandy Heller? Sanford Heller?"

"The one and only."

"Developer, entrepreneur, and sleazeball," I said.

"Exactly."

"He owned half of Jersey, last time I looked."

"The last time you looked must have been a while ago," she said. "I'm pretty sure he owns the whole thing by now."

Sandy Heller was New Jersey's answer to Donald Trump, except that he was even oilier, sleazier, and more in love with himself. He was also tougher than Trump. Trump had been given a head start in life by the fact that his father was a millionaire developer himself. Heller was entirely self-made.

"Joanna's mother was one of the saddest creatures anybody's ever laid eyes on. She was a graduate of Radcliffe, a journalism major. By the time she was twenty-five, she was writing for *Life* and *Time* and *Newsweek*. And this was back in the days before women's liberation. She met Joanna's father while she was doing a story about corruption in the real estate business. Sandy *was* corruption in the real estate business—still is—but I guess he has a kind of charm, or a kind of crude brute strength, because she fell for him, and they got married. But when he married her, he made her agree to give up her career."

"Why?"

"I don't think it was because he was old-fashioned. I think it was just because he was a narcissist. He didn't want anybody outshining him in any way. He had always surrounded himself with small people, and he took some perverse pleasure in finding a woman who wasn't small, and making her small."

"And Joanna got away?"

"She was in college when her mother died, and as soon as it happened, Joanna just cut her ties with him. She wouldn't take his phone calls and she wouldn't take his money. She was a kind of debutante during her first two years of college, and then she became one of us: working, taking out loans."

"You admire her."

"I admire her deeply. Her whole life had been a kind of devil's bargain: she could have all the wealth in the world, and all she had to give up was...not her soul, but her autonomy. Her father was willing to put her through Radcliffe only on the condition that she wouldn't get a job after she graduated. He said it would demean him if people knew that his daughter was working. As if people would think he couldn't support her."

"What a jerk," I said.

"That's Sandy Heller."

"Is Joanna close to her brother?" I said.

Sandy Heller had a son, Eric, who was not only the heir apparent to the family business, but was often mentioned as a future presidential candidate. He was known to be a shrewd and often ruthless businessman, and, unlike his father, he was personable and well-spoken. He was only in his early thirties, and had never run for office of any kind, but there was a certain indefinable buzz about him. People were always predicting a great future for him, if he were to choose to go into politics.

"I doubt they're close," she said. "I very much doubt it. He's the apple of his father's eye. I doubt he would do anything his father didn't want him to do. At least that's the impression I have."

"So what's her life like now?"

"For a long time it was a great life. She works for a foundation, raising money for children who don't have health insurance, and she married a great guy. Ben is really a special man."

"What does he do?"

"He's a dean…somewhere. He used to be a dean at Rutgers. But after they split up he moved to Oregon or Washington or something. He's working at a college out there. I'm spacing on the name."

"Do you know why they split up?"

"Their lives fell apart. They had a child, a beautiful boy named Cody. Cody was born with a blood disease. I don't know the particulars. All I know is that he had to have transfusions every two weeks. They took him to hospitals all over the country. They kept thinking they were going to find a cure. And they never did. Cody died."

"Do you happen to know where he was being treated when he died?"

"I think it was Sloan-Kettering."

I almost said "Bingo," out loud. But I hadn't simply learned something that constituted an important piece of a puzzle. I had learned about the death of a child. So as I absorbed the new information, and thought about what it might mean, I did so in silence.

I asked a few more questions about the Liptons, but I had found out what I needed to know. After a while I called for the check.

"You should really visit once in a while," she said. "Harry misses you."

"I miss Harry."

The waiter showed up and I gave him my credit card.

"One last thing. Do you happen to know where Sandy Heller lives?"

"I'm not sure. It's not New Jersey. It's somewhere in Connecticut. I know it's Connecticut. But I don't know where."

"Would it be Westport, by any chance?"

"Westport. That's it. Westport."

## Chapter twenty-five

Sandy Heller's home phone number and address weren't listed, but the World Wide Web came to the rescue once again. If you have access to the Internet and you're willing to spend a few bucks, there's almost nothing you can't find.

I tried to call him at his home the next morning. The phone was answered by a Latina woman who spoke perfectly good English but who passed the phone to someone else, a man with an Eastern European accent so thick it sounded as if he was putting it on. He said that Mr. Heller wasn't available and that the Liptons weren't staying there. I asked him his name and he wouldn't give it to me. When I told him I'd call back later, he told me not to call back at all.

He didn't tell me not to visit, though.

I drove up to Westport in the afternoon. Heller's home was just a little bit smaller and less conspicuous than the Taj Mahal. It was set far back from the road and high on a hill. At the entrance to the driveway there was a security booth with a man inside. There was a high stone wall around the property. I saw at least one surveillance camera. Presumably there were others.

It would be hard to get in there.

It would even be hard to scope the place out. A guy sitting in a Mustang, leafing through books on the art of forgery, was not going to remain unnoticed by the police or by Heller's private security for long.

I drove back down to New York, went to my office, checked my mail, checked my email, and tried to think.

Kate came by to take care of some odds and ends. I filled her in.

"So you think Mrs. Lipton is staying at her father's place? Even though she hates him?"

"Maybe she's somewhere else in Westport. Who knows? But for the moment, that's the working hypothesis."

"So what are you going to do?"

"I'm going to figure out a way to get in there."

"How?"

"I'm not sure."

"Maybe you could pretend to be a pizza delivery man."

"The success of that plan," I said, "would depend on their ordering a pizza."

"You have so many things to teach me," Kate said.

I was thinking, though, that Kate was not far off. Maybe I could dress up as a meter man, or a phone repair guy. I had done such things before, and it had usually worked. Except I'd never tried an act like that to get into a place as heavily guarded as the Heller residence was likely to be.

I called Beth and asked her for Joanna's cell phone number.

"I don't have it. We're really not that close."

"Well, do you think you could do me a favor? Do you think you could call her at her father's place?"

"I don't have the number there either."

"I do."

"You got hold of Sandy Heller's private number?"

"I did."

"Resourceful. Resourceful as ever, Singer. I'm impressed."

"Resourceful enough to get the number, but not quite resourceful enough to get anybody to talk to me. Except some Bulgarian guy who won't even take a message."

"A Bulgarian guy?"

"I use the word Bulgarian just to be colorful and specific. The guy who answered the phone had an Eastern European accent. I don't know where he was actually from."

"Colorful, specific, and ethnically insensitive."

"I don't know what's so insensitive about calling somebody a Bulgarian, but anyway…do you know who this guy is?"

"I don't know him in particular. I do remember that even back in the day, Joanna talked about how her father employed people from the Russian mafia to do his dirty work."

"The Russian mafia," I said. "Oy."

"Oy?"

"That's a Yiddish term that, in this context, means, 'I better not forget to bring my Uzi.'"

"I've heard they can be pretty tough customers. It would probably be prudent to avoid them."

"They *can* be pretty tough customers. But then again, they've never come up against the Battling Jew from Jersey."

"That would be you?" Beth said.

"That would be me. So. I've got Heller's number, and I'm thinking that Joanna Lipton might be staying there, and I think you might have a shot at actually talking to her if you called her there. So can you call her?"

"Yes. I'd be happy to."

"Thanks," I said.

"Don't thank me. If Joanna *is* staying with her father, it's a sign that something is seriously wrong. I can't think of anything that would make her want to go back to him. So I'd be calling not just for you, but for me. I want to find out if she's OK."

❧

Beth called me back a little later.

"Well, I spoke to her."

"And?"

"She says she's fine, but she doesn't sound fine."

"How does she sound?"

"I can't really define it, but she sounds strange."

"Did you ask her why she's staying in Westport?"

"Turns out she's not in Westport. She's at the cabin."

"What's the cabin?"

"She and Ben bought a place in the Adirondacks around the time Cody was born. They always called it the cabin. It's actually the size of Greenland, but they call it the cabin. Anyway, she's there. It's in a town called Black Brook."

"So how did you track her down there?"

"When I called her father's place, I left a message for her with your Bulgarian friend, and he had her call me back."

"He likes you more than he liked me."

"Evidently."

"Did you get her number up there?"

"No. I'm sorry. She's never given out their number. She always talked about it as the place she went when she wanted to get away from the world."

"Nothing on your Caller ID?"

"I don't have Caller ID."

"Did you get any sense of whether she was alone there?"

"She said she was. But I don't know. She sounded weird."

"Weird like maybe someone was standing next to her while she talked to you?"

"Maybe. I don't know. Maybe."

"Thanks," I said. "I owe you one."

"Not really," she said. "Just make sure she's all right."

⁂

It took me a few minutes to get the address of Joanna Lipton's place in the Adirondacks. I got directions on Yahoo. It was a six-hour drive. I made coffee, poured it into a thermos, and got going.

When I take a long drive for pleasure, I listen to music or books on tape. During this drive, I didn't listen to anything. I'm not sure I can explain why. I can't say I was preparing for what I was about to do, because I didn't know what I was about to do. I suppose I was just trying to get focused.

It was raining when I left the city. As I approached Albany, a hundred and fifty miles to the north, it was five degrees colder and it was snowing. By the time I reached the Adirondacks it was snowing heavily. The car kept skidding, and I kept having trouble turning into the skid. I knew that that's what I was supposed to do, but it was hard to do it. My impulse is always to fight the flow, not to go with it.

The snow slowed me down and what was supposed to be a six-hour drive took ten.

I stopped for gas in the village of Mercer and got some more coffee and a prepackaged sandwich in the snack shop. I also bought a map. I still had my directions to the cabin, but I thought a map of the surrounding area might come in handy.

By the time I got to Black Brook it was dark and, as the radio informed me, I was officially driving through "blizzard conditions." The roads were becoming impassable, and I was doing about five miles per hour. Finally, going by the map, I calculated that I must be within a quarter-mile of the cabin. I parked the car, got my tool kit and my gun out of the glove compartment, and walked the rest of the way.

I was wearing waterproof boots, and I like the cold, so I thought I wouldn't mind the walk. But the snow was coming down crazily in thick fat flakes, and within a few minutes I was covered in a layer of snow and my face was stiff and stinging.

I could barely see through the thickly falling snow. The next time I had to make a stealthy approach to a murder suspect during a snowstorm, I would remember to bring goggles.

The cabin was more like a compound. It was surrounded by a

brick wall about ten feet high. On a normal night it wouldn't have been difficult to find a way over it, but this was not a normal night. I couldn't get enough of a grip to scale the thing. The next time I had to climb a brick wall in order to make a stealthy approach to a murder suspect during a snowstorm, I would remember to bring a ladder.

I could have gone to the front gate to see if I could get it open, but the chances of being spotted would be much greater there—as would be the chances of triggering a sensor-activated floodlight or walking into the line of sight of a security camera.

The property was surrounded by thick woods. At least they looked thick to me, but then I'm from New Jersey. I turned back and walked among the trees, searching for something, anything, that might help me deal with the wall. To occupy the part of my mind that was screaming about how cold it was, I tried to remember the words of "Stopping by Woods on a Snowy Evening."

It took me about half an hour, but finally I found a group of large flat rocks that I could arrange on top of one another. I carried them over to the wall, one by one. This was a drawn-out process, because I kept slipping in the snow. But finally I had them arranged so that I could stand on them and get my hands on the top of the wall. Though I could hardly feel my fingers, I managed to get a grip on the top of the wall and pull myself up.

The top of the wall was wide, more than a foot across, so I was able to sit there, trying to determine if that vantage point could enable me to see anything I wouldn't be able to see from the ground. But I couldn't see a thing. The snow was too thick. I couldn't see the cabin at all, though I knew it was there.

I let myself down on the other side of the wall and walked without having any idea what I was walking toward. I spent a few minutes wandering in the darkness, wondering if I was going around in circles. The next time I had to make a stealthy approach etc., etc., I would bring a compass.

Finally I saw lights. The lights of the cabin. I'm not sure it's even accurate, though, to say that I saw them. It was more like I sensed them, a faint glow in the whiteness of the blizzard at night.

I made my way up to the place. I couldn't really see it clearly until I was almost at the front door. There were lights on in the second floor but not in the first.

I didn't know if Joanna Lipton was alone, and even if she was alone, I didn't know if she'd want to talk to me. So I didn't bother to ring the bell. I tried the front door, but it was locked. I walked around the house and found a side door and a back door, but they were locked too.

At the back door I unzipped my overcoat and got out my tool kit. I had everything a well-appointed second-story man could want: a pen flashlight to see the lock—a super-duper halogen model that could burn holes in your eyes if you weren't careful; a cigarette lighter to heat the lock sufficiently for me to get a pick in; lubricant to oil the mechanism of the lock; and, of course, a wide variety of picks. I used the lighter and then the lubricant, and kept the flashlight in my mouth while I worked on the lock.

It took me about five minutes, but I got in.

In order to get the snow off my boots, I would have had to stamp my feet for half an hour or so, which would have been loud, so instead I took them off in the hall.

I made my way slowly up the stairs. The television was playing. I could hear the unmistakable voice of Captain Picard: "Damage report, Mr. Worf."

I don't think I can describe the feeling of satisfaction that you get when you've been working on a case that has troubled you and you know at last that you are about to get to the bottom of it. I don't know if I thought that Joanna Lipton had killed Dr. Carpenter with her little red sports car, but I was convinced that once I started talking to her, I would find out what I needed to know. I was convinced that even if she hadn't done it, she had the key.

Since I didn't know if she was alone, I had my hand on my gun. But I didn't bring it out of my pocket, because if she was alone, happily watching *Star Trek*, then coming in with my gun drawn would not be the approach best suited to encourage her to trust me.

I was next to the doorway. I pushed the door open.

"Aren't you gonna say something like, 'Grandma, what big teeth you have'?"

Lee Macy was sitting in an armchair. He was aiming a shotgun at my head.

"Take your hands out of your pockets very slowly, asshole," he said, "and put them on your head."

I did as he suggested.

"I think I figured something out," I said.

"What's that?"

"You're mixed up in this whole thing."

"I'll send a letter to your next of kin to let them know you were a good closer. You went out with a very accurate deduction." He pointed the shotgun at me. "You're right, Singer. I probably wouldn't be sitting in this godforsaken place freezing my tits off if I didn't know that you were going to come poking around."

I was trying to stay calm, but it's hard to stay calm when you're standing just a couple of feet away from someone who is ill-disposed toward you and holding a shotgun. I was reminding myself to take long, deep breaths, because if you can remind your body not to lapse into an automatic fear response, you have a better chance of controlling your fear. This was something I'd once learned from a book of meditation. Maybe it was Jon Kabat Zinn's *Wherever You Go, There You Are*. It's not the kind of thing you're going to admit to your detective friends, but in a moment of mortal peril I was trying to calm myself down by remembering the teachings of a Buddhist self-help book.

"Why are you here, though?" I said. "Why are you protecting Joanna Lipton?"

"Is that the way you think it's going to go, Singer? You think this is a James Bond movie? Where the bad guy spills his guts to the good guy while he's holding a gun on him?"

I shrugged my shoulders. "I thought I'd give it a shot."

"Not the way it happens," he said. "The only thing I *am* going to tell you is that I've been sitting here laughing at how easy this all turned out to be. When I made her tell your friend that she was up here, I knew you'd be coming for a visit. But when I saw the weather report I was afraid you might be sensible enough to wait a couple of days. I don't know what I would have done. But this is just perfect. After I kill you I can put your body under fifteen feet of snow. There's a gully about a quarter mile from here that'll do just fine. Nobody's going to find you till the spring, and by that time they won't even be able to tell it's you."

He chuckled about this, shaking his head with disbelief about how easy this was turning out to be. I tried to calculate what my chances would be if I rushed him. He was still pointing the shotgun at me. My chances wouldn't be so good.

Holding the shotgun in his right hand, he walked up to me and frisked me with his left. He took out my wallet and gun and put them on top of a chest of drawers. Finally he found my tool kit, which was in the side pocket of my overcoat. He flipped it open and looked at it with derision.

"What's this? Your little bag of tricks? You get this in a catalogue from *Boy Detective* magazine or something?"

He tossed it into a wastepaper basket in the corner and shook his head with contempt.

"You weenie," he said. He gestured toward the door with the shotgun. "Let's move," he said.

I headed toward the stairs.

His gun had caught my attention. It was slim, elegant-looking, not the kind of thing you'd expect to see in the possession of a macho guy like Macy. Because my brain is a treasure trove of more or less useless information, I even knew what make it was. It was a Winchester 254, a rifle marketed to women. Light, attractive, with delicately molded grips. For when you want to blow somebody's ass away with a feminine touch.

"Are you out of the closet, Macy? That's a mighty cute gun."

I was looking to rattle him in any way I could. Looking to distract him, if only for a second.

"I found this here while I was waiting for you. It must be Mrs. Lipton's. I thought it'd be poetic justice to kill you with this thing.

This is the second time I've met you, and both times, you were a wuss. I kicked your ass in your office and now I'm going to kill you. I out-muscled you and I out-thought you. And because you've been such a fucking girl, because you've been my bitch, I'm going to kill you with the gun that seems just right for you right now. That way I don't have to use my service revolver and I don't have to use my back-up."

I hadn't succeeded in distracting him.

He opened the rifle at its hinge and looked down its barrel to make sure it was loaded. Then he flipped the safeties so it was ready to be fired.

He motioned me toward the back door. My shoes were sitting on the mat.

"Don't bother to put your shoes on," he said. "You won't need 'em."

"You're going to march me to the fucking gully and you think I'm gonna do it without shoes? Fuck you. Shoot me here, asshole."

He decided not to argue. "Put the shoes on," he said.

I put the shoes on and we went outside. It was still snowing like crazy.

Something was working in my memory, but I didn't know what it was.

What is the mind? It was a philosophical question I couldn't pursue at the moment, but it's endlessly strange that a person, a self, seems to be composed of many different voices, emanating from many different regions. What I'm trying to say is that one faint voice in some far-flung region of my mind was working hard to get a message through to the central consciousness.

"Something about you brings out the Jew-hater in me, Singer. I never knew how much I hated Jews before I met you. And I can't help feeling a little bit of pleasure about the fact that I'm marching you somewhere right now. It feels so historical. Didn't they used to march your kind into the woods and shoot you, before they came up with the gas chambers?"

"Kiss my ass," I said. Capable of witty banter to the last.

We trudged through the snow, which was nearly knee-deep.

It was horribly quiet. Nothing except the sound of the wind as the snow fell silently.

Something kept tugging at my memory. I still didn't know what it was, but I finally knew what it was *about*. It was something about the wussy rifle he was going to shoot me with.

When I first became a field investigator, after they moved me out of the research room, I scrupulously and painfully schooled myself in the subject of firearms, their modes of functioning, their history, their lore. I wanted to know my way around guns, and my way of going about it was to read about them endlessly and spend as much time as I could on the firing range. Before that, I had never had an inkling that different guns not only had different uses, different purposes, but they also had different personalities and temperaments. It was something I never learned to give a shit about—unlike someone like Macy, who believed that he was making a statement by killing you with one sort of gun rather than another—but after a while, there was no homicidal maniac rifle buff in the world who knew more about this crap than I did.

Reading about firearms brought me a great deal of knowledge that was never practical, that I could never put to use. But now, as we pushed through the wind and snow toward what was presumably my final destination, I finally understood the message that my memory had been trying to tell me. Macy might not know how to use that gun.

The Winchester 254 was developed as part of a marketing campaign to make hunting seem more appealing to women. It only worked with special bullets, which had been designed to remind women, on an unconscious, subliminal level, of tubes of lipstick. I remembered reading about it at the time it was manufactured.

But I also remembered reading that the rifle had had to be redesigned after it was out on the market, because it was attractive and so easy to handle that it was being used by little kids. The original model had featured a triple safety system, but after an eight-year-old boy had figured out how to disengage all three safeties and killed his brother, Winchester had redesigned it with yet another safety: a lock that was hidden in the handle and that could only be opened with a key. It was just another example of the basic moral goodness of capitalism: rifle-makers going that extra mile to make it a little bit harder for the youth of America to blow their families away.

If I was remembering right, only a few of these new and improved models ended up being sold before Winchester decided that the marketing strategy wasn't working—they just couldn't get women that interested in hunting—and they phased out the whole line.

The chances were good that Macy didn't know any of this. He might know it if he were a rifle buff, but on the other hand, he might not know it even then: even a rifle buff might not have bothered to read about a weapon designed for women. If he'd spent any time fooling around with the rifle before I arrived, then he surely would have figured it out. But maybe he hadn't.

It was snowing harder than ever. I could barely see.

"Not much further, asshole," Macy said.

I didn't know whether the gun was one of the late model Winchesters, with the hidden safety, or one of the earlier models, without one. If I tried to take it away from him, he might be unable to fire, or he might put a hole in my chest. But sometimes you have to take a chance.

"Hey Macy," I said. "Never fuck with a scholar." Those could have been my last words.

I turned around and rushed him. He pulled the trigger. I was moving too quickly to be terrified; if my life was flashing before my eyes, I was too intent on flattening him to notice.

He pulled the trigger but the rifle didn't fire.

I plowed into him. I didn't hit him as hard as I'd wanted because I couldn't get any traction in the snow, but I got my shoulder down and rammed it into his chest at the same time as I put the heel of my palm on his chin and snapped it back. Macy probably could have braced himself if he'd chosen to, but instead he tried to shoot again, and again nothing happened.

We landed in the snow, me on top of him, and I put my knees on his chest and hit him in the face three or four times. I heard bones breaking, and hoped they weren't in my hand. Between the cold and the adrenaline, I couldn't tell.

I'd hit him hard enough to put most people out, but Macy was a hardheaded bastard, and although blood was popping up out of his face in little geysers—from his nose, from his mouth—he had the presence of mind to work his hand up around my throat. Once he had it there he started to squeeze my Adam's apple as hard as he could. I hit him with two more rights to the face but the strength of his grip didn't diminish. He got his other hand up and began working with his thumb, trying to gouge my eye, but, thanks to the blood in his own eyes, he couldn't see that well and couldn't quite do it.

I kept punching and he kept squeezing. One of his hands, his left hand, disappeared. I didn't look, but I could tell that he was hunting around for something in his pockets. I pinned his left arm with my knee. He worked it loose. I pushed myself off him just in time. He was holding a long knife—he had pushed the button and popped out the blade and lifted it into the air. He caught me on the hip, slicing me just as I was moving away. I scooped up the rifle and ran. He knew the house better than I did, so I didn't run toward it, but in the opposite direction. I was betting that the cocky bastard hadn't taken the trouble to do a thorough survey of the surroundings. He had probably just sat there waiting for me in the warm house, drinking beer and watching ESPN.

I heard a shot. When you hear that sound there's a moment in which you wonder whether this is it, whether you're about to die. I kept running and felt nothing, and a moment later heard the bullet hit a tree. I crossed up over a slope. When I got to the other side I knew I was out of Macy's sight for at least a second. There was a small cottage, a guest house, not too far away. I made for it as fast as I could, which wasn't very fast in the knee-high snow. It was like running in a dream, trying to go fast but barely moving. I heard a few more shots, which told me that he was shooting blind—the night was dark, the snow was thick, and I'd done a job on his eyelids—but also that he had enough ammunition to waste some.

Soon the only sounds I could hear were those I was making: my feet crunching in the snow, my hectic breathing.

I ran to the back of the cottage and tried the back door. It was locked. I smashed a window with the rifle butt. I wanted to be inside, so I could look out at the night without having the snow impede my vision. It wasn't just that the snow was so thick that it was hard to see through; it was so thick that it was hard to keep your eyes open all the way.

I climbed in and, moving quickly to the front of the cottage, stood flat against the wall next to one of the front windows. I looked outside. I thought I saw something moving, but between the darkness and the swirling snow, I couldn't be sure.

I had a loaded rifle in my hands but it was useless to me.

If I'd had my fucking tool kit, I could have sprung the lock on the rifle in two seconds. I didn't know if I was going to be able to find anything in this place that I could improvise with.

There was a desk in the corner of the room. Top drawer: papers and envelopes. Shit. Middle drawer: calculator, dental floss, Rolodex, cigarettes. Shit, shit, shit. Bottom drawer: pens and paper clips. Maybe.

I pushed the desk away from the wall and crouched behind it. On short notice it was the best I could do for a fort. I straightened out a paper clip and inserted it in the lock. The room was pitch-dark, but that didn't matter. If I was going to be able to pick the lock, I wouldn't need light—you do it by touch, not by sight. And if I wasn't going to be able to, then light wouldn't help.

I had to keep telling myself to slow down. I was afraid that Macy was about to just walk in and shoot me but the worst thing you can do is rush yourself. Picking a lock is a delicate job. Although I was as scared as I'd ever been in my life, I forced myself to go slow, slow, slow.

The front door of the cabin slammed open. Macy had kicked it in, and was standing in the doorway holding a hand gun.

I was still fiddling with the paperclip. I felt the tumbler responding. I turned the lock.

Macy switched on the light.

I pointed the rifle at him.

"You moron," he said. "It didn't work for me—you think it's gonna work for you? You think it likes you?"

Because he had a gun in his hand, I didn't waste any time with repartee. I just shot him.

The bullet hit Macy in the chest and he fell back with an expression of astonishment. He hit the wall, hard.

He wasn't dead yet, though. He hadn't even fallen down. I don't know what animals the Winchester company thought women were going to hunt with these things: muskrats? possums? mice? He still had his gun in his hand. I shot him again.

He slid down the wall. He was struggling horribly for breath. His body was struggling, at least. I don't know if his brain was connected anymore.

I stood over him. His chest was torn apart.

I shot him a third time.

That was it.

# Chapter twenty-six

I sat beside his body for a long time, fighting off the desire to be sick.

I have never killed except in self-defense, but the first time I ever killed someone, I felt as if I had lost my soul. If I were a religious man, I might believe that I was doomed to spend eternity in hell for having killed. And there are times, in fact, when I do believe this, even though I am not a religious man.

I must have lost only a part of my soul that first time, because whenever I have killed since then, I have felt that old feeling, but even worse. Maybe I've lost a deeper and more precious region of my soul each time. Or maybe I did lose my entire soul the first time, and in the times since then I have been burning up karma, losing the souls of lives that haven't even been lived yet.

It was only after ten or twenty minutes that I remembered that he had knifed me. I remembered this because it began to hurt. I went to the bathroom and washed off the wound. It wasn't deep. Mostly he'd just ruined my clothes. I couldn't find proper bandages, so I just put a washcloth over the wound.

Macy had told me that he was going to throw me into a gully. I left the cottage and tried to retrace my steps. It wasn't easy, in the blinding snow, but after half an hour or so I was able to find the spot where we'd fought. He'd sliced off part of my overcoat with his knife. I hadn't even noticed that it was missing until I found it there in the snow.

After this, I was oriented, and so I walked in the direction where we'd been heading before I'd turned around and rushed him. After ten minutes I found the gully. I walked back to the cottage and carried his body there. I'm strong, but he was heavy, and I had to stop many times along the way. It was a ten-minute walk that took me an hour. For the first few minutes there was an uncomfortable intimacy involved in carrying the body of a man I had killed, but after a while I just started to hate him for weighing so much.

If you want to make your life unhappy and short, one of the best things you can do is kill a cop. Macy was a crooked cop, and I'd killed him in self-defense, but it would be time-consuming to establish these things, and even if I did, his colleagues would do their utmost to make me wish I'd never been born. This was why I was carrying him. I wanted him in a place where he wouldn't be found for a long time.

When I reached the gully, I laid him on the ground and took another look at his face. It seemed to have hardened during the walk. I don't mean that the stiffness of rigor mortis had set in. I mean he looked somehow meaner in death than he had in life. He looked as if he wanted to come back to life and beat more people up.

It was a thirty-foot drop to the bottom of the gully. I could have just rolled him over the side, or kicked him, but I didn't think any man deserved to be kicked into his final resting place, not even a man like Macy. I picked him up again, and tossed him over the side. The snow on the bottom was so thick that I barely heard him hit.

I had his knife and both of his revolvers in my overcoat pocket. I threw the knife and the police service revolver in after him. I kept his other gun, the gun he'd called his back-up. I was sure it was unregistered: it was the gun he used for his dirty work. He'd probably taken it off some unfortunate perp long ago. I thought it might come in handy to have an unregistered gun.

I also had his wallet and his keys. I took out his driver's license and made a mental note of his address. Then I put it back in the wallet and threw the wallet into the gully. I held onto the keys.

I trudged slowly back to the cottage and cleaned the blood off the wall and the floor. Then I picked up the rifle and went back to the main house. The snow was finally tapering off. I was exhausted, and it took effort to drag my legs out of the snow at each step. A few hours earlier I had expected to die, and the fact that I was still alive made everything I looked at seem to shimmer. The sheer mystery of being alive was—I was about to say that it was intoxicating, but in fact I had never felt more clear. A man was lying dead less than a mile away, a man who had been somebody's child, and I was exultant. The snow was finally tapering off, the moonlight was falling strongly through the trees, and I was alive.

At the main house, I cleaned the rifle and replaced it in the rifle-rack. There were other rifles in it, and none of them had hidden safety locks. If he hadn't wanted to make a statement with the *way* he killed me—if he'd just wanted to kill me—then I'd have been dead by now.

I went upstairs, retrieved my wallet and gun and tool kit, cleaned my wound again and bandaged it properly this time.

It was four in the morning, and I was as tired as I'd ever been in my life. It was a pretty sure bet that no one was going to interrupt me here, but I knew I wouldn't be able to sleep. So, without any enthusiasm for the task, I left the house again and walked to my car. By the time I got there it was dawn, and the snowplows were already out. They are very efficient about these things in the Adirondacks, where snowstorms are an everyday occurrence. I got on the road and drove back down toward the city, stopping once for breakfast, another time just for coffee, another time to buy clothes. The things I was wearing were waterlogged and stinking.

Before I went anywhere else, I stopped by Macy's place. It was in a large apartment complex in a quiet part of Queens. I rang the doorbell to make sure no one was there, and then I let myself in.

The apartment looked like a drill sergeant's quarters. It was spotless and Spartan. There were no paintings, no ornaments of any kind. There was one large bookcase, filled entirely with books on military history. He seemed to have a particular interest in the Second World War.

I looked slowly and thoroughly through his things. Aside from a few pornographic magazines and videos, there was little evidence of a personal life of any kind.

I turned on his computer and was glad to find that it wasn't password-protected. After clicking around for a while, I found what I was looking for.

Macy had been a meticulous record-keeper. In one financial program, he kept track of his salary, his bank accounts, his 401-K plan, his IRAs. In another, he kept track of revenue from freelance work—legitimate freelance work, like moonlighting as a bodyguard for politicians. And in a third, he kept track of revenue that was not the kind that you reported to the IRS. He had noted his earnings from several different sources. It turned out that Sandy Heller was only one of a number of businessmen who had availed themselves of Macy's services.

Some of the headings in this ledger were rather colorful. Muscle, for instance, was a category that included payments as well as earnings. Macy had listed the names of several subcontractors, including Carl Packer (more fondly known to Kate and me as the Soup Dragon). Packer had received a large payment the day after Kate and I had entertained him in her apartment. There were about ten other payees, the names of some of whom I recognized as New York City policemen.

Another, even more colorful category in Macy's ledger was "Wet Jobs." The phrase "wet job" is a term of art for a contract killing. Macy had been paid for wet jobs on two people. The first—five months ago—was someone named Henry. The second was me.

It might or might not have been stupid to keep records of

this kind. Macy had probably liked having records that he could use against his employers, should that become necessary. And it never would have occurred to him that his own record-keeping might be used against him. He'd been nothing if not cocky.

Anyway, he'd been right. They never would be used against him now.

In his desk I found a flash drive. It was about the size of a fingernail clipper, and I was able to save every piece of information on his computer on it, with room to spare. The wonders of the modern world. I put it in my pocket.

After that, because I like to be methodical, I went through his apartment again. I came across with some interesting items, but nothing else that related to the work he'd done for Heller.

In a desk drawer he had a pair of handcuffs and a key. I put them in my pocket. He also had bullets that fit his unregistered gun. I took them too.

There was nothing more to be done there, but I remained for another half hour. Is it too mystical to say that the silence in the home of someone who has just died is deeper than any other kind of silence? And is it too mystical to say that if the person who has died is someone you have killed, and you are alone in his home—among his books, his clothes, and the other common objects of his life—the silence is like no other silence you have ever known?

I didn't regret his death, since the alternative had been my own. But it seemed important to stay there for a while. In going so thoroughly through his apartment, I'd found no evidence that Macy had cared about anyone, no evidence that anyone had cared about him. So it was easy for me to believe that simply by remaining here in the silence for a while, I would be giving him the last true expression of respect he would ever receive.

I drove to my bank and put the flash drive in a safe deposit box that I keep there. Then I made some sketchy notes about what I'd learned so far, and I put them in the safe deposit box as well.

Then I drove home.

I was exhausted, but I couldn't sleep. I thought of calling Kate, just to talk, but stopped myself. I didn't want to become dependent on anyone, and even if I *had* wanted to, she was the wrong person to become dependent on. She was a girl in her twenties. It would be selfish to ask her to absorb what I was feeling: the guilt, the moral nausea, that comes with having killed a man. The kinds of things I would have said to her were things you only tell your lover, your shrink, or your bartender. It wouldn't have been fair to ask Kate to carry all that.

I sat on my living room couch and read for a while. I was reading the letters of Anton Chekhov. He was one of the writers I turned to when I wanted to remind myself why I was alive and why I do the work I do.

"My holy of holies," he wrote in one letter, "is the human body, health, intelligence, talent, inspiration, love, and absolute freedom, freedom from force and falseness in whatever form they express themselves."

Finally I succeeded in falling asleep, and didn't wake until the evening.

# Chapter twenty-seven

As soon as I woke, I dressed, got in my car, and drove to Westport. I parked near the foot of Sandy Heller's driveway. A kid who looked like the young Elvis was manning the security booth. Sort of. Mostly he was listening to something on his iPod and leafing through the latest issue of *Guitar Player*. He glanced up and started to say something and I just walked past him, toward the house. The driveway was long enough to provide me with my quota of exercise for the day. By the time I got there, two men had come out of the front door and closed it behind them.

One of them was tall, with a squarish head and a squarish suit. His face had seen its share of trouble. His nose was mashed flat against his face and there was thick scar tissue around his eyes.

The other one was rather small and lithe. I got the impression that despite his size and slimness, he was someone who could handle himself. He seemed very calm.

"May I help you?" he said.

He was the man I had spoken to on the phone. The man

who, according to Beth, probably had a connection to the Russian Mafia.

"I want to speak to Joanna Lipton."

"Joanna Lipton does not reside here," he said. "This is the home of Sanford Heller."

"I know that Joanna Lipton doesn't reside here. But I also know she's here right now." I knew no such thing, but it never hurts to act as if you know what you're talking about. "And I would be grateful if you would let her know that if she won't see me now, she'll be receiving a visit from a contingent of New York's Finest within the hour."

He looked at me steadily. I had five inches and probably about fifty pounds on him, but he did not appear to be intimidated.

It was beginning to occur to me that getting past Macy might have been the easy part.

"I'm sorry," he said. "Mrs. Lipton cannot see you."

"All right," I said, and turned back toward the street.

In movies by John Woo, the Hong Kong director known for the "balletic" violence of his action scenes, you can tell the good guys from the bad guys even during the most confusing shootouts because the good guys always have guns in both hands. During these shootouts, there are often a lot of doves fluttering around, for some reason. I didn't expect to see any doves tonight, but in every other way I felt like the hero of a John Woo movie.

This was because I reached into my overcoat pockets and brought out a gun with each hand. Macy's gun was in my left hand, trained on the block head of the blockheaded giant, and my own gun was in my right, trained on the smaller man.

"As I mentioned, I want to see Mrs. Lipton now."

Neither man moved.

The fact that someone had tried to kill me the night before had put me in a bad mood.

"I swear to you that I will kill you both."

Somehow, the little man was unfazed. "If you insist," he said, "please come in."

He seemed completely calm, as if he'd merely lost one battle in a war he was confident of winning.

We entered the house and walked down a hall until we reached the living room. A woman in her mid-thirties was sitting by herself on the couch.

"Joanna Lipton?" I said.

She turned toward me, with a visage as mournful as any I'd ever seen in my life.

"I've heard you've been looking for me."

"Do you know why?" I said.

"Yes," she said. "I know why."

She spoke in a very soft voice.

"I'd like you to come with me," I said.

"Why?"

"I want to talk to you, and I get the feeling it would be easier to talk without your friends here listening in."

I was still aiming my guns at them. The larger man looked as if he would like to rip me limb from limb. The smaller man looked dapper and nonchalant, as if he didn't care at all about what was happening. But he was very watchful. He didn't take his eyes off me, and I was sure that if I relaxed my concentration even for a second, he would pounce.

"Let's go," I said.

"May I just get my bag?"

"I would prefer it if you didn't. Just come with me. We can get you your bag later."

I wanted to be far away from the small man as soon as I could.

Joanna Lipton seemed spiritless, defeated. She didn't seem to care much whether she left or stayed.

We started to head toward the door. I was walking backward, still aiming a weapon at each man.

The choreography of this was going to be awkward. My car was parked on the street, and Sandy Heller's driveway was roughly the same length as the Saw Mill Parkway.

"If I have to walk backward all the way to my car," I said, "I'm going to get a crick in my neck. So here is what I would like you to do. First, lie down on the ground."

Neither of them did anything.

"You should know that I won't hesitate to kill you. If you have any doubt about that, give your friend Lee Macy a call."

More silence. No movement. The large man didn't seem to understand what I was talking about. Finally the small man nodded slowly and lay on the floor, and the large man followed suit.

"Good. Now. Scoot on over to the bottom of the stairs and lie back to back."

The smaller man looked annoyed. It had taken a while to get a reaction out of him, but the reaction was still pretty mild. He looked the way he might have looked if I'd beaten him at Parcheesi.

The larger man was breathing heavily with anger. He was snorting a little, like a bull.

I put one pistol into my overcoat, reached into my breast pocket, and took out Macy's handcuffs. I put the handcuff on the smaller man's right wrist—precisely because he was so much calmer, I knew he was the more dangerous of the two—ran it around the bottom leg of the banister, and then handcuffed him to the other man.

The banister had been built back in the day, when they did things right. It was a massive oaken thing. "That should keep you for a while," I said.

I knew that it might not actually keep them for long, but it would give me time to get Mrs. Lipton into my car. That was all the time I needed.

I felt a touch of satisfaction knowing that the only way they were going to free themselves was by marring Sandy Heller's exquisite banister. Probably that would get them in trouble with the boss. If the things I'd heard about Sandy Heller were true, the fact that they couldn't stop me from messing up his property would annoy him even more than the fact that they couldn't stop me from taking away his daughter.

"Handcuffs are about twenty dollars a pop these days," I said, "so I'd appreciate it if you could get these back to me after you're done with them."

I took Mrs. Lipton by the arm and hustled her out of the house and down the driveway. Elvis was still in the security booth, still listening to his iPod. He noticed us only as we were passing, and looked amazed. I saw him get on his phone.

I helped Mrs. Lipton into my car, got in myself, and took off.

She hadn't said a word. I was wondering if she was drugged.

I didn't say anything until we were on the highway.

"So here's my question," I finally said. "Did you kill Andrew Carpenter?"

She didn't say anything.

I took that as a yes.

"All right," I said. "So *why* did you kill him?"

She still didn't say anything. I drove five miles, ten. I wasn't sure what I was going to do with her. But finally she spoke, and once she had begun, she didn't stop.

"I had a child," she said. "A boy named Cody. He was the gentlest, most loving boy you'll ever meet. But he was never strong. He was born with a condition called thalassemia. It means that you can't make healthy blood cells. My ex-husband and I are both carriers, but neither of us knew it until Cody was born."

She was speaking very softly. It was hard to hear her, but I didn't ask her to speak up. She was in a fragile state, and I was afraid that if I interrupted her, even just by asking her to talk louder, she wouldn't be able to keep going.

"Cody had his first blood transfusion when he was three days old, and after that he had to have transfusions every three or four weeks. I don't think I can make you understand what it's like to watch your infant child suffering the way Cody suffered. He needed the transfusions. He needed them to stay alive. But they were hell."

I was looking straight ahead at the road, checking the rear-view mirror often, in order to make sure that we weren't being followed, but at the same time I felt as if every fiber of my being was concentrated on the effort to hear her.

"Cody was the friendliest little boy in the world. We would take him into the hospital and he'd be smiling at the nurses, playing peek-a-boo, and suddenly one of the nurses would put a tourniquet around his arm and another would be applying disinfectant and preparing the needle, and suddenly these people who had been playing with him were hurting him, and his mother—his *mother*—was standing by and letting them do it. How can a little baby make any sense of that?"

I was starting to see where this was going. Or maybe I had seen where it was going a while ago, before I had even met her. But I hadn't been sure until now.

"The only therapy for his condition is blood transfusions. But blood transfusions come with serious side effects. A few years of transfusions and iron overload begins. It will kill by the age of fifteen if it's not treated. The only way to treat it is to hook your child up every night to a machine that delivers a medicine that slowly reduces the iron in the body over a ten-hour period. You do this at home. So every night you plunge a needle into your child's arm and tape it down to make sure it doesn't come out while he sleeps. After he reached his second birthday, my Cody spent six nights out of every seven hooked up to a mechanical pump. If he woke up early, he couldn't just play in his crib like other children, because he knew he wasn't supposed to dislodge it."

I wasn't sure she was aware of me any longer. She had wanted to tell all this to someone; that was clear. I just happened to be the person who had asked.

"And then we met Dr. Carpenter. The magnificent Dr. Carpenter. He was called onto the case to treat the damage that the iron overload was doing to Cody's heart, and he ended up taking over Cody's care. And he was the first doctor who gave us hope. We'd gotten used to the idea that there was no cure for our son's condition, but that if we kept treating him and administering his medicine conscientiously, then we could keep him alive. He had an illness that he was going to have to live with all his life, but it was an illness that he *could* live with. He could have a happy and satisfying and maybe even a long life. But Dr. Carpenter said he could do more for Cody. He said he could make him well. He told us that there was a new medicine, not yet on the market, that could cure our son's condition once and for all.

"What were we going to do? Say no? Insist on going over the data from the research studies? He was a well-respected doctor. Everyone we knew told us he was the best. When he had us sign the consent forms, he added all the proper qualifications. He told us that there were no guarantees, that the drug was experimental, that it could end up not working, that there were risks involved with any medication. He told us all that. But he exuded a sense of confidence. Even when he read us the list of warnings, he read it in this tone that made you feel sure that it was just a silly formality, because nothing could really go wrong.

"I know that it's our fault as much as his. We were supposed to be sophisticated people, people who know how to be effective advocates for their children. But we were dazzled. He was a star. So we did what he told us to do.

"For a few weeks, the treatment seemed to be working. Cody's red blood cell count was rising for the first time in his life. We were in heaven. If Andrew Carpenter had told us that there was a religion built around worshiping him, we would have joined.

"And then the treatments stopped working. I can't describe to you how heartsick we were when Cody's red blood cell count started dropping again. We thought we should go back to the blood trans-fusions. But Dr. Carpenter told us to wait. He told us to 'stay the course.' Those were the words he used. He said we were in a war for Cody's life and we had to stay the course. So we did. We trusted him. And Cody got worse and worse. He didn't look like himself dur-ing those last few weeks. His face was round and puffy and yellow. His eyes were yellow. He started to grow hair on his face from the steroids they were giving him to counteract the effects of the other medications. And Dr. Carpenter came around each day, and he kept telling us to 'stay the course.' So we stayed the course, even though it should have been clear to us that the course was leading straight to Cody's death.

"After he died, my husband and I blamed ourselves. We didn't blame Dr. Carpenter. It should have been obvious that Cody spent the last two weeks of his life dying in front of our eyes. It should have been obvious that if we'd taken him off the drug there would have been a chance to save him. And it *would* have been obvious, to anyone in the world—anyone except people like us, *sophisticates*, so dazzled by our doctor the star that we stopped being able to think for ourselves.

"Ben and I broke up not long after Cody died. You might think that an experience like that would bring two people together. But after Cody died, every time we looked at each other…"

We were drawing close to Manhattan. Mrs. Lipton hadn't asked me where we were going. She had no idea where I was taking her, but didn't seem to care. She was still inside her story.

"About six months ago," she said, "I heard some things about Dr. Carpenter."

"What sort of things?"

"Conflicts of interest. I learned about it from people I trust. They said that Dr. Carpenter was on the board of a drug company, and that he'd come under suspicion for promoting drugs that were produced by that company when there were other drugs that were safer and more effective."

She looked up at me. She looked as if she were angry at me, though I hadn't said a thing.

"Do you think I'm being paranoid?" she said. "Do you think I'm just looking for someone to blame?"

"No," I said. "I've heard about Carpenter and Weatherall Pharmaceuticals."

"Weatherall. That's right. That's the name of the company. Those bastards." She hadn't cried before, but now she broke down in loud violent sobs. I thought she was going to cry for a long time, but she stopped herself with great effort. She still had more to say.

"Evidently he was careful," she said. "No one could put him on trial, no one could touch him. But as soon as we heard about it, we knew what had happened to our child."

"You said that you learned about Carpenter and Weatherall six months ago."

"Yes. What about it?"

I didn't say anything.

"Why did I wait so long to kill him, you mean?" she said.

"That's what I was wondering."

"It was an accident. Well, not exactly an accident, but it's not like I'd been planning to kill him. I used to fantasize about it, but I never considered really trying to do it."

She looked over at me and laughed.

"What's funny?"

"I was about to say 'I hope you believe me,' but then I realized that I don't really give a damn if you believe me or not."

"For what it's worth," I said, "I do believe you."

"Why?"

"Because of what Beth Palmer has told me about you."

"Whatever. Whether you believe me or not, this is what happened. I was visiting a friend who was recovering from breast cancer treatments. The last thing in the world I wanted to do was set foot in Sloan-Kettering again, but she's a good friend. I spent the morning with her, and after I left I walked back to Second Avenue, where I'd parked. I remember how pleasant the day was. I got into the car. And that's when I saw him. He was with three other people, a man and two women. The man and one of the women got into a cab, and then he walked with the other woman for a little while and said goodbye to her at the light.

"The woman he was walking with—I knew she wasn't his wife. He had a picture of his wife in his office and I'd looked at it many times—she's a beautiful woman. This was someone younger. They were flirting. I won't pretend to know whether they were sleeping together, but they were flirting. What anyone does with his private life is his own business. But what flipped the switch in my mind was the sight of how much he was obviously *enjoying* himself. My Cody's ashes are scattered all over the Long Island Sound, and his killer was out walking in the sunshine, flirting, enjoying the day.

"And I still don't know if I would have done what I did if I hadn't made up a little story in my mind about the couple. The couple who'd just gotten into the cab."

"You imagined they were the parents of a child who was under Dr. Carpenter's care. They were putting their trust in him, and they had no idea that he was going to kill their child, too."

She looked up sharply. It was as if she was taking notice of me, for the first time.

"How the hell did you *know* that? How did you know that's what I was thinking?"

"I don't know," I said. I didn't. "And?" I said.

"And I decided to hit him with my car. It was insanity, but I'd never felt so sane in my life. At first I think I put my foot on the gas just to tease myself. Like I was saying to myself, 'You could do this. It would be possible to do this.' And then somehow I crossed a line, and knew that I really *was* going to do it. I just put my foot on the gas and did it. And you know what? The impact was horrible—I have nightmares about it, the way it sounded and felt, and I think I'm going to have nightmares about it for the rest of my life. But after I did it, I was glad. I didn't know if I'd killed him, but as I was driving home that night, I was glad."

I glanced over at her. She was looking at me with fierce, burning eyes.

"You must think I'm a monster."

"I don't think you're a monster."

"Well, the fact is, I don't care if you do. I killed him. I killed Dr. Carpenter. But *he* killed my Cody. And tell me, Mr. Private Detective—where in the world are you going to find another baby like my baby? Where in the world are you going to find another boy like him?"

## Chapter twenty-eight

It seemed indecent to keep pressing her after that, but there still were things I needed to know.

"And then?" I said.

"Why does there have to be an 'and then'?"

We were in the city now, on Riverside Drive.

"You have this thing," she said. "I've only known you for half an hour and I already know you have this thing. When I ask you a question, you don't say anything. What is that?"

"I don't answer questions that you know the answer to. There has to be an 'and then' because there were a lot of different choices you could have made after you killed Carpenter. I probably would have killed Carpenter myself, if he'd done to one of my children what he did to yours. I know I would have wanted to. But after I killed him, I would have made different choices from the ones you made. Maybe I would have turned myself in to the police. Maybe I would have just gone about my business as if nothing had happened. You didn't do either of those things. Instead, you ran to a father you despised, and when I started looking into Carpenter's killing, your father sent his goons out to kill me."

She said something, but too softly for me to hear it.

"What's that?" I said.

"I wanted to turn myself in."

"What stopped you?"

She didn't say anything.

"I think I can guess," I said. "You changed your mind because your father advised you against it. When you realized what you had done, you had your moment of elation, and then you panicked, and you went to your father. Why you went to him, I'm not sure. But in the moment of truth you turned to your father, and your father decided to throw a cloak of protection over you. Before you knew it you were in Westport, under a very elegant form of house arrest, and the investigation was finished, and miraculously no one had called you or linked you to it. You began to think that it was all over, that you might get away with it after all. And you tried to convince yourself that it would be fine to get away with it, because you hadn't committed a crime: all you'd done was bring Carpenter to justice for killing your son. But you've been tortured about it ever since then, and you know that the only way you can live with yourself is if you turn yourself in, but either your father has stopped you or you're so afraid of him that you haven't even tried."

I had gotten off Riverside Drive was heading east.

"You got some of it wrong," she said, "but you got a lot of it right."

"Which part did I get right?"

"My father does not want to see his daughter go to jail. He says it would be very bad for his business. And it would be the end of my brother's political career. He told me that those things are too important to sacrifice."

"Which part did I get wrong?"

"My father didn't just advise me against going to the police. He stopped me. He stopped me from leaving his house. He stopped me from using the phone."

"You took Beth Palmer's call."

"Nicholas was standing right next to me. He'd already told me what I had to say, and he was standing there to make sure I'd say it. I couldn't understand the point of telling Beth I was up at the cabin."

I didn't bother to tell her what the point of it was.

"So what was his plan? To keep you locked up there forever?"

"My father has never let me in on his plans," she said. "He isn't about to start now."

"Does your brother know about all this?"

"I have no idea. And I want you to know that I had no idea about any of the things you've been talking about. That anyone tried to hurt you or your friend."

"I know that," I said.

"What are you going to do? Are you taking me to a police station?"

"Not right now," I said. "Maybe later."

"Where are we going now?"

We had passed through Central Park at 96th Street and were now on the East Side.

"I'm not taking you to a police station because I'm not working for the police. They never asked me to look into Dr. Carpenter's death. In fact, they were annoyed when I started. I'm working for Natalie Carpenter, and my responsibility is to her. Mrs. Carpenter is sure that her husband was murdered, but no one will believe her. She deserves to know the truth. I have no opinion about whether you should tell your story to the police. But I want you to tell it to her."

"Are you sure that's the best thing for her?"

"Yes. I am sure."

I called Mrs. Carpenter from my cell phone and asked her if I could come over. I said that I'd be bringing someone with me, someone who would tell her things she needed to know.

She sounded sober, composed. I don't think I would have taken Mrs. Lipton there that night if she hadn't.

I parked on East End Avenue, a block north of Mrs. Carpenter's townhouse. It was a warm evening, but Mrs. Lipton was trembling uncontrollably as we got out of the car.

Mrs. Carpenter was alone in her apartment. I introduced the two women.

"I know you," she said to Mrs. Lipton. "I know you...but I'm not sure from where."

"I think we've attended some of the same parties," Mrs. Lipton said.

We sat in the living room.

"Mrs. Lipton has some things to tell you," I said. And then, to Mrs. Lipton: "Please take as much time as you need."

She spoke slowly and softly, without any evasions. She told Mrs. Carpenter everything she'd told me. She spoke about her son's illness, about her relief when Dr. Carpenter took over Cody's care, about her growing doubts after Dr. Carpenter put Cody on the experimental medication and Cody failed to respond. She spoke about Cody's death, and about what she felt when she heard rumors that Dr. Carpenter had come under suspicion for his relationship with Weatherall.

As I sat there watching them, I felt a rising admiration for both women. Joanna wasn't faltering. Now that she had decided to tell her story, she was telling it without any apparent hope of being forgiven. She understood that Mrs. Carpenter needed to know the whole story, and so she told it, evenly and slowly.

I don't know when Mrs. Carpenter realized where the story was heading. Maybe she knew as soon as we arrived. She listened calmly. She was looking not at Joanna but at the floor. When Joanna talked about Cody, about what a beautiful boy he'd been, Mrs. Carpenter's face was shining. When Joanna talked about Cody's illness, the glow of Mrs. Carpenter's face was even more moving, because now the glow came from her tears. And when Joanna began to speak about her growing doubts about her son's treatments, and then about the rumors that Carpenter had let his own financial interests override his medical judgment, I expected Mrs. Carpenter to grow defensive or hostile. But instead, her face took on an ever more somber cast. She looked tragic and beautiful.

During the hour in which Joanna talked and Mrs. Carpenter listened, I think I fell in love with both women.

At one point my cell phone rang and I recognized the caller as someone I needed to talk to. I took the call in the kitchen. After I got off the phone, I started back toward the living room. I could see them at the end of the long corridor, and, without quite knowing why, I stayed where I was.

I stood there for a long time, watching them, without being able to hear the words that were being said. I knew that Joanna had reached the end of her story when I saw Mrs. Carpenter step over to the couch where Joanna was sitting, sit down beside her, and embrace her. I stood there in the hall, looking on, as the two women wept in each other's arms.

# Chapter twenty-nine

I went back into the kitchen and poured a glass of water. I was sitting at the kitchen table drinking it when Mrs. Carpenter came in.

Her eyes were still bright from her tears. Her face, her whole being, was suffused with a kind of tragic seriousness.

She sat down next to me at the table.

"That's quite a story," she said.

"It is."

"I need time to think."

"You've got all the time you need."

"I asked her to wait in the living room for a little while—said I needed to talk to you. Do you think you could spend a minute helping me sort things out?"

"Of course."

"I never knew much about Andrew's professional life," she said. "I knew there were some problems with a couple of the drugs Andrew was prescribing, but I thought he was one of the people who helped bring the problems to light. I thought it was the drug company that was dragging its feet about admitting that the drugs weren't working. I didn't think it was Andrew.

"But you want to know what the strange thing is? The strange thing is that I believe her. When she was telling me about how her son got sicker and sicker, and Andrew kept telling them to stay the course, I could hear him saying it."

I could too. His assistant had told me that it was his favorite expression.

"I want to find out if the things she was saying about the medication Andrew was using are true," she said. "But it feels like a formality. I know in my heart that they're true."

"Are you sure?"

"Andrew was a brilliant doctor. He was also the most driven man I've ever met. The most ambitious man. And not the man most likely to admit his mistakes."

I nodded. It was the picture of him I'd formed from conversations with other people who knew him.

"What happens now?" she said.

"That depends on you. If you want her to be arrested, all you have to do is call the police. I can make the call for you. The decision is yours."

"What do you think I should do?"

"I'm just a detective," I said. "I'm not a moral philosopher."

"I thought that when you found the person who killed Andrew, I would want to make sure he spent the rest of his life in jail. But now…I don't know what I want to do."

"There's no need to decide now. You've got time."

She put her head in her hands.

"I could never have imagined that I would meet the person who killed Andrew, and feel sorry for that person. But I feel sorry for her."

"You're a generous woman."

"The only thing I'm sure of," she said, "is that I can't linger over this. I can't sit here for weeks with this woman's fate in my hands. Whatever I decide, I need to decide soon. I need to sleep on it, if I can sleep. And then I need to decide before the sun goes down tomorrow."

"I think that's a good idea."

I stood up.

"Are you all right by yourself here tonight?" I said.

"Yes," she said. "I'm all right."

"Let's talk tomorrow then."

I went down the hall to get Joanna.

# Chapter thirty

I don't know how you can be proud of a person you've just met, but I felt proud of you in there." I said this to Joanna as we were walking toward my car. "I felt proud of both you," I said.

"I wish I could be proud of me," she said quietly.

We got into the car and I started north up East End Avenue.

"What happens now?" she said.

"What happens now is up to her. She needs to decide what to do with what she's learned tonight. She might choose to inform the police, and she might choose not to."

"And if she doesn't?"

"If she doesn't, she doesn't."

"You won't tell them either?"

"No. I won't."

"What kind of a private detective are you?"

I shrugged.

"Aren't you guys all ex-cops?" she said.

"I'm not an ex-cop. I'm an ex-English student. If you read

too much literature, you start to see moral ambiguities all over the place."

She laughed. It was the first time I'd heard her laugh.

"What's funny?" I said.

"The thought that somebody who used to be a literature student could leave Nicholas and Joseph lying on the floor like that, handcuffed. My father's never going to believe it."

"What's the story with Nicholas and Joseph?"

It would be nice to think I'd seen the last of them, but I didn't, so I thought it was time to start finding out who they were and what they were capable of.

"They're both from Russia. My father had a pipeline to the Russian Mafia years before anybody knew there was a Russian Mafia."

"Which one is which?"

"Joseph is the big one. He's just a bodyguard. He's been with my father for about five years. He never talks, he never smiles. He just likes to hurt people. Once some college boy threw a pie in my father's face while he was speaking at a conference. I think he was protesting one of my father's housing projects—my father was tearing down a beautiful old working-class neighborhood to put up a luxury high-rise. Anyway, the boy who did it was a skinny college kid, and I don't think he even hit my father with the pie. He missed. But after Joseph was through with him, you would have thought he'd gotten tortured by the KGB for stealing state secrets. There was no reason to be so rough on the boy. But Joseph just enjoyed it."

"And Nicholas?"

"Let's put it this way. Of the two of them, Nicholas is the one who really frightens me."

"He frightens you how?"

"He's very smart, for one thing. And he's always very composed. You saw how calm he was, even when you were putting the handcuffs on. Joseph is someone I could imagine going on a rampage and hurting many people. Nicholas is someone I could imagine planning a mass murder. He would do it in the most efficient, most rational way, and then he would go home and eat dinner."

We had reached the George Washington Bridge, and were about to cross over to New Jersey.

"Where are we going?"

"I'm taking you to my home. There's a spare bedroom. You'll be safe for the night."

"It's not going to work, you know."

"What won't work?"

"Your whole plan. If you have one. You've been talking as if Natalie Carpenter's decision is going to mean something. But it isn't. Do you think my father is going to let it play out the way you think it's going to play out? Do you think my father is going to let people find out what I did?"

"He can't stop it."

"Of course he can stop it. He's going to find us. And they're going to kill you. I don't know what they'll do with me. But I know they're going to kill you. Nicholas is going to supervise it, and Joseph is going to do it. Or maybe Nicholas is going to do it himself this time, because he won't be able to stand it that you made him look bad."

"They didn't do too well against me the first time."

"You don't know my father. Those two don't really matter. You could kill Nicholas and Joseph, and my father would send a thousand Nicholases and Josephs after that. And then he would send another thousand for every one of *them*. My father doesn't want the world to know what happened. Not because he's trying to protect *me*. There's just too much at stake for him to let it come out. He's been grooming my brother to become president since he was born. The president can't have a killer in the family."

"I suppose it's high time I talked to him," I said. "Perhaps by reasoning with him we can appeal to his faculty of enlightened self-interest."

"You're kidding, right?" she said.

"I'm talking fancy, but I'm not kidding. What I'm saying is that he needs to know that if he keeps trying to cover this up, he's going to lose. The more he fights this, the worse it's going to get for him." I got out my cell phone. "Call him for me, please."

She took the phone and made the call.

"Yes, it's me," she said. "Yes, I'm with him now."

She handed me the phone.

"Singer? Are you there?"

"I'm here, Mr. Heller."

"You're a pain in the ass, Singer. You're a complete pain in the ass."

"Thank you," I said.

"You understand, I hope, that I'm going to crush you. You've been annoying me, but you're annoying like a fly is annoying. You're history. You're a dead man already."

He had a grating voice. He sounded like the love child of a bullhorn and a duck.

"Do you have much more of this?" I said. "How about I put you on hold for five or ten minutes and when you're done ranting, we can talk?"

"What the fuck do you want to talk about, Singer? There's nothing to fucking talk about. You're dead."

"Well, yes, in the long run, that's true, but the point right now is that I've got you cold. You lost. I had an encounter with one of your employees the other day, after which I paid a visit to his apartment. Unfortunately, he was an idiot, and he liked to keep meticulous records about the funds he was receiving and what he was receiving them for. The records are safe, in a place where you can't get them. Right next to the records are my notes about this case. I figured out what happened to Carpenter before I paid my visit to your house this evening. If I die, the first thing that happens is that friends of mine open the box."

"I might take you seriously, Singer, if I believed one fucking word you were saying. But I don't. I don't believe in your fucking safe deposit box."

"You're not going to win this, Mr. Heller," I said. "Even if you do something as indecorous as kill me, you're still going to lose. At this point I suggest you stop thinking about how you can silence everyone who knows about his, and start thinking about damage control. Public opinion in America is very forgiving. Nothing as trivial as a slight case of manslaughter is going to stop your son from being president someday. It might even help."

"Fuck you, Singer," he said. "I'm not going to lose. I never lose."

And he hung up on me.

"That went well," I said to Joanna.

We drove on in silence for a while. Then she said, "Indecorous?"

I shrugged. "It's the way I talk."

# Chapter thirty-one

I had a cleaning woman at my place once a week, so it looked respectable when Joanna and I arrived.

There was a fold-out couch in the study. It wasn't the most comfortable thing she could have slept on. There was a twin bed in Wini's room and another in Jack's. But the kids' rooms were sacred.

Joanna sat at my desk, drinking a glass of water—it was all she wanted—while I converted the couch into a bed and fitted it with sheets and a blanket. I got out towels, a basket of fresh toiletries, and a sweatshirt-sweatpants combination that Claire had won at a charity raffle at Jack and Wini's school and never worn.

"You're very well prepared," she said. "It's like you're running a B&B here."

"There's a washer-dryer in the basement," I said. "I can wash your clothes tonight if you want, or you can, or else we can just buy you some things in the morning. There's a mall a few miles up the highway."

"Is that one of the things a private detective does? Accompany women to the mall?"

"It's a big part of the job. But not one that we like to publicize."

The house is a rambling thing, a Victorian from the 1930s that Claire fell in love with just before Wini was born. So after Joanna went into the study and closed the door, I was able to pace back and forth through the first floor, perhaps talking to myself on occasion, without worrying about whether I was disturbing her.

I was more nervous about this whole thing than I wanted to admit to her.

At about three in the morning I was at the kitchen table, drinking coffee, when Joanna appeared. She was wearing Claire's sweatsuit.

"You're still up," she said.

"I'm still up."

"You haven't been to bed at all."

"Not yet."

"I haven't been to sleep either."

"Couch isn't comfortable?"

"It's not that. I've been thinking."

"About what?"

"I've probably been thinking the same thing that you've been thinking."

"Which is?"

"That my father probably isn't going to let go without a fight."

I nodded.

"He's going to try to kill you," she said.

"That goes without saying."

"Do you think he's going to try to do anything to Mrs. Carpenter?"

"Not immediately. Getting rid of me will be his first priority. Getting you back will be his second. After all that's been accomplished...yeah. He'll probably want to do something about her too."

"And me. You said he'll want to get me back. Do you really think that's what he wants to do with me? Just get me back?"

"You'd be in a better position to answer that than I would."

"I don't think my father cares about anyone. I don't think he cares about anything except power. Getting it and exercising it. He kept me locked up because he didn't want the truth of what I did to come out, and also because he couldn't figure out what else to do with me. Right now I think he's probably decided that keeping me locked up like that is too risky. Because even if you're out of the picture, someone else like you might come along. I think what my father will do is kill you, and put me back under house arrest, as you called it. And then, after some time has passed, I think he'll find a way to make sure that Mrs. Carpenter and I disappear. I think he'll find a way to make her death and mine look like accidents. No one will ever connect us. No one will ever have any reason to think that our deaths had anything to do with each other."

"That sounds about right to me."

"Jesus," she said. "I can't believe it's come to this." She was sitting in a childish posture: both of her feet on the seat of the chair, with her chin resting on her knees. "I've always known that my father has no morality. And I've probably always known that if he wanted something, he would never let anything or anyone stand in its way. But I've never really understood before that that includes me. I've never really realized that if he considered me an obstacle to something he wants, he wouldn't hesitate to have me killed."

She looked stunned by what she had just said, what she had just thought. "I feel numb. Like I'm having a stroke or something."

"You're not having a stroke," I said.

She had just figured out that her own father was likely to try to kill her. Inside every person alive, there remains somewhere the primal conviction that one's father is the most powerful presence on earth. The part of her that was an adult was probably already speculating about the possibilities inherent in the situation—how her father would move against her; how I might try to stop him; what information she might have that could help me stop him—but the primal soul of her was sure that because her father wanted to kill her, she was going to die.

Private detectives in the movies are always coming into contact with gorgeous and glamorous women, and always bedding them. The truth is more pedestrian. Some of the women you come into contact with *are* gorgeous and glamorous. But they're gorgeous and glamorous at other times in their lives. When I encounter them—Mrs. Carpenter, weeping in my office; Joanna, benumbed with fear at my kitchen table—they are not really women anymore. When I encounter them, circumstances have turned them into the defenseless girls they were when they were small. My job, you might say, is to change the circumstances of their lives in order to help them become women once again.

"So what do we do?" she said.

"There's only one way to stop your father from trying to cover up what you did. He can't try to cover it up if you've already confessed to it."

She looked relieved. It was clear that she wanted to confess not just to Natalie Carpenter, but to the world.

"I have a friend who writes for *Newsday*," I said. "Addie Stone. She's a good woman. I think she can help us."

"How? Why not just go to the police?"

"We need to go to the police eventually, but, as I know from personal experience, your father had a friend in the force. That particular person won't be troubling us, but I have a hunch that there might be more where he came from. I wouldn't want to usher you into the waiting arms of somebody else your father has bought and paid for. If Addie writes up your story, it will insure that nobody from the police will try to hush it up."

"Addie Stone it is, then," she said. "How do we get hold of her?"

"We call her."

"Now?"

"I can leave a message on her voice mail at work. She'll pick it up first thing in the morning."

I picked up the phone and heard a dial tone, and then it was gone.

And then the lights went out.

"This," I said, "is the problem with living in the suburbs."

"Blackouts?" she said.

"I wish."

The electricity and the phone lines weren't connected, but they had gone out at the same time. This meant there was more than one person outside.

"We need to move fast," I said.

I got out a steak knife and put it in my belt. Then I led her quickly up the stairs.

"What's going on?" she said.

"Your daddy's friends were listening."

I was whispering.

"What?"

"They're outside. They're here."

My cell phone was in my bedroom. I dialed 911. Nothing happened.

I'd put my gun and Macy's gun in my closet. I got them out and jammed them into the side pockets of my pants. The knife was in my belt and the flashlight was in my back pocket. I'd never be able to wear these pants again, except for lounging around the house, but this was not a prime concern at the moment. I also got out my flashlight.

"I have to go downstairs," I said. I was still whispering. "Stay here. If they get past me, they're going to find you. Not much we can do about that. Let's just hope they don't get past me."

There was of course a chance that they'd enter by the second floor instead of the first, but I didn't think they would. Wherever I waited for them, there was a chance I'd be guessing wrong; I just had to go with my best guess.

I started for the door. She clutched my arm. She looked frantic, and to prevent her from saying something our friends could hear, I put my hand over her mouth.

She nodded to show she understood that she had to be quiet, and I took my hand away.

She spoke in a whisper. "Why? Why are you going downstairs? You could just stay here and shoot at them if they try to get in."

"They could wait us out. They could wait for a month. Do it in shifts. The longer I delay, the more time they have to get in position."

Or to place a bomb, I thought, or start a fire. I saw no need to mention these possibilities to her.

I left the room and walked quietly down the hall. At the top of the stairs I waited, listening, trying to hear if anyone was in the house.

I couldn't hear anything. I went downstairs as quietly as I could. Which wasn't very. Each stair creaked in its own way.

There was no one in the house yet.

The basement door was in the downstairs hallway, between the living room and the kitchen. I stepped behind the door and closed it, leaving it open just a crack.

I was more frightened than I wanted to admit to Joanna. More frightened, in fact, than I wanted to admit to myself. I didn't know how many of them were out there, and I didn't know what equipment they had with them. I knew they must have night vision goggles—otherwise cutting the electricity wouldn't make sense, because in my house, in the dark, I'd have them at a disadvantage. But I could only guess at what other high-tech toys they might have. Cutting the electricity and the phone lines was old hat, but jamming the cell phone was impressive. I knew it could be done, but I'd never *seen* it done before.

I was standing in the closet, the door opened just a crack, and I was no longer a human being. I was a mixture of fear and a strange, pure curiosity. What were they doing?

Fear, curiosity, and readiness.

One of the living room windows was being jimmied open. Whoever was doing it was skillful.

Skillful, but a little slow. My eyes were fully acclimated to the dark now. By moving so cautiously, they'd squandered some of their advantage. If they'd just stormed in and started blasting holes in the place before I'd had a chance to think, I'd be dead by now and they'd be dragging Joanna to their car to take her back to Westport.

Even though I was still scared, I started to sense the growth of a beautiful and familiar confidence. These guys had already made one mistake and we'd barely gotten started.

The window was wide. Two men came through at once. They were wearing thick black clothing: bulkier than footfall uniforms, slimmer than spacesuits. Which meant that they were wearing Kevlar: they were bulletproof from head to toe. They were both holding long thin pistols, doubtless equipped with many space-age accoutrements.

All I had were two revolvers, a kitchen knife, and a flashlight.

They were both wearing helmets—fitted, maybe, with night vision lenses alone, or maybe with motion and audio sensors thrown in. Which would mean that while I stood behind the basement door, unmoving, being as quiet as I could, they could quite possibly be hearing every breath I was taking, and were about to begin firing a few hundred rounds of ordnance through the door.

One of the men was much taller than the other. I couldn't see their faces—they could have been Abraham Lincoln and Napoleon, for all I could make out. But I knew. Of course they were Joseph and Nicholas.

I had my gun in my hand. Macy's gun was still in my belt. That John Woo shit—a gun in each hand—wouldn't work in this situation. If you're firing two guns, all you can do is blast around wildly. Against men with bulletproof vests, I needed to be precise.

Their bodies were protected by the Kevlar, their faces by the helmets. My task was to shoot both men in the throat.

I'm a good shot, but those were small targets and there were two of them. And they'd be moving.

Stay calm. Stay calm. Don't fire wildly. Fire calmly.

I thought: *You can do this. You can do this.*

They looked through the living room, and then started toward the kitchen. The way they were looking reassured me that they weren't using any fancy sensors.

It occurred to me that their high-tech toys might actually be another mistake. Night vision goggles are all well and good, if you're accustomed to wearing them. If you're not, they can just as easily be an encumbrance.

With my left hand I got the flashlight out of my back pocket. It was the halogen flashlight, a super-high-intensity little mother.

The corridor was narrow, so they walked in single file, with the larger man, Joseph, in the lead. The basement door, behind which I was concealed, was halfway down the corridor. I waited until he was close to the door. Then I kicked it open, pressing the button on the flashlight and thrusting it into his face. With my other hand I jammed the barrel of my gun into his neck and fired. The second man had stumbled when I rushed them. Now, with Joseph falling back against him, they were a tangle of bodies. I was able to reach around and fire a shot. I tried for Nicholas's torso—I had no hope of getting him in the throat. He was thrown back toward the living room, but remained on his feet. He'd been hit somewhere in the body. The Kevlar protected him, but getting hit by a .45 at close range is kind of like getting hit by a linebacker. I walked straight toward him, firing off shot after shot. I shot him in the body and I shot the helmet. The helmet didn't break and I couldn't succeed in hitting him in the fucking throat. He stayed on his feet but kept being thrown backward. Although his gun was still in his hand he hadn't yet fired. Even a man who feels no sentimental aversion to killing and little fear of being killed can choke when the moment of truth arrives. I was out of bullets so I got out Macy's gun. Nicholas raised his weapon but I was close to him now. I grabbed it with my left hand and shot him in the wrist. The gun fell out of his grasp. I grabbed his jacket and attempted to find his neck so I could put a hole in it. He punched me in the stomach, a short sharp stinger that doubled me over and would have been much worse if the force of it hadn't been muffled by his glove. Then he hit me on the side of the head with some sort of karate move. I fell to the floor. The fact that I was dealing with Nicholas, someone for whom I'd formed such an instant antipathy, was a piece of information that shouldn't have helped me in the least, but somehow did: it *personalized* this. Not only did I not want to be killed, I did not want this arrogant bastard to kill me. I somehow got up quickly—not a simple feat, with my world spinning—and ran toward him, my head down. My hazy plan was to get my head under his and use the top of my skull to butt his unprotected chin. This didn't work. He kicked me as I came toward him and I went down again. I was on my knees.

And that was when I could have died—should have died, if he'd been going about his job properly. But instead of choosing efficiency, he made the mistake of choosing style. Rather than picking the gun back up and shooting me, he decided to kick me again, and decided to do it with a fancy move involving a three-hundred-and-sixty-degree twirl. Although it was a twirl that would have done Michelle Kwan or Peggy Fleming proud, Michelle Kwan and Peggy Fleming don't actually win many fistfights. Before the kick could land I'd had time to get out the knife, and I drove it as hard as I could into his left thigh. He didn't go right down, but his fancy kick was ruined: instead of hitting me in the head, he hit me harmlessly on the shoulder. With my left hand I took hold of his pants in the crotch area and with my right I drove the knife in even deeper. When the sounds he was making convinced me that he was in sufficient pain I removed the knife and punched him in the throat.

Pinning him down wasn't difficult—I must have outweighed him by fifty pounds. If I'd had my wits about me I would have merely subdued him. Instead I used the knife again, forcing it into his throat, and I kept twisting it as violently as I could. He was struggling underneath me, and then he stopped struggling, and I kept twisting the knife, because even if he was dead already I didn't want to stop, even if he was dead already I wanted to kill him more thoroughly. In the state of temporary insanity that you have to be possessed by in order to kill a man, I think I actually believed that there were different degrees of deadness and I wanted to make sure that he was not merely dead, but very dead. Blood was everywhere, and his legs kicked wildly and then weakly, and then more weakly. He was like a troubled marionette, a marionette trying to run in its sleep. Then his legs stopped kicking, and the blood was still spraying everywhere, and somehow I was still pushing the knife, and then I stopped, finally, because even if there *were* different degrees of deadness, he had reached the last of them.

I rolled off him. Using my sleeve to wipe some of the blood from my eyes, I checked his friend Joseph, who was still lying inertly where he had fallen. I looked for a pulse; there wasn't any.

I sat on the floor. My head felt like a music box. It took me a minute or two just to remember that Joanna was still in the house.

I went up the stairs and knocked on the door of the study.

"It's me. We're OK."

I opened the door slowly. I knew she'd been terrified, and I didn't want to barge in there.

She was in the closet. She reminded me of pictures I'd seen of children in London during the blitz. Hollowed out and shell-shocked.

"What happened? What's happening?" Her voice was shaky and small.

"We're OK." I would have liked to say something witty, but I couldn't think of anything witty to say. It's only in the movies, really, that people make witty remarks just after they've killed somebody.

"I can get you a drink if you want one," I said. "But I think it might be a good idea for you to stay up here for a little while."

"Why?"

"It's kind of messy down there."

"I think I need to see," she said.

"No you don't. Trust me."

"This was all because of me. I need to see it. I need to know what happened."

She made her way down the stairs. I would have preferred if she'd stayed on the second floor until the cops came, but I didn't try to bar her way.

She reached the living room.

"That's Nicholas," she said.

My head was still achy and heavy and light.

"I know," I said. "He had some nice moves. He should have been a dancer."

She saw Joseph lying in the corridor.

"How did you do this?" she said.

"I surprised them."

"You surprised both of them?"

"Yes."

"But these men are trained killers."

I didn't say anything, and then she looked at me with a changed expression, as if a new truth had dawned on her.

"I guess you are too," she said.

# Chapter thirty-two

I knew a few people on the police force in town, one of whom, Clem Turner, was on the night squad. He was a good man, someone I knew I could trust. He arrived within twenty minutes, with a team. Beat cops, detectives, lab technicians, EMS people.

"You gotta excuse the crowd," he said. "But we don't usually get this kind of excitement around here."

I didn't have to make the case that I had killed these men in self-defense. Their outfits made it kind of obvious.

After I had told him what had happened, Turner moved to the question of why it had happened.

"I have a feeling these guys didn't just choose your house at random. It's probably not like they just happened to be driving by and decided to try out some of their stuff."

"Probably not," I said.

"So they must have thought they had some reason to pay you a visit."

"Must have."

"And you probably know what that reason was."

I didn't want to tell him the reason. I wanted Joanna to have a chance to tell her story to Addie Stone before dealing with the cops.

I wanted her to talk with Addie because Addie would write about her with sympathy. I didn't want the world to condone what Joanna had done; I wasn't hoping that she could avoid serving any time in jail. But I wanted the world to understand what she'd done, and what she'd been through. Addie, I thought, might be the difference between Joanna serving a fair sentence, and Joanna getting locked away for fifteen years.

I had just finished making coffee, and I poured him a cup.

"If I did know—I'm not saying I do know, but if I did know, and you asked me about it, I guess I'd have to start talking about standards of confidentiality observed by a professional investigator like myself."

"Of course. But then again, if you did that, I guess *I'd* have to start talking about the fine professional standards of cleanliness and safety that we observe in the city jail."

I knew I didn't need to take that seriously. Clem would have liked to know why these guys were here, but he wasn't going to put me in jail for refusing to tell him. If a cop has to investigate a killing, then Clem was dealing with the kind of killing that every cop wants. No unidentified bodies, no vanished killers, no messy tangle of evidence to sort through. All he'd have to do is write it up and go to sleep. He knew the who and the how, which were the important things; he would have been interested to find out why, but it wasn't essential.

It was about six in the morning when he flipped his notebook closed and stood up.

Joanna had been sitting in the corner quietly. Now she spoke.

"I don't think you should go yet. I think I have a few things to tell you."

"You don't need to say anything, Joanna," I said.

"The way you've been relating to this man makes me think that I can trust him," she said. "Is that right?"

I had known Clem for almost ten years. He was a good cop.

"You can trust him. Yes."

"Then I think it's time," she said.

Clem took his notebook back out, put it on the coffee table, and sat down.

"I'm listening," he said.

# Chapter thirty-three

I don't know how to thank you," Mrs. Carpenter said.

We were in my office. She wrote out a check and handed it to me. It was for twice the amount we'd agreed on.

"This'll do," I said.

When I had first met Mrs. Carpenter, I had known that she would be beautiful again someday. And today, she *was* beautiful again. But probably not in the way she had been before I met her. I'd seen old photographs in her apartment, and she now had a kind of gravity, a kind of austerity, that she'd never had before.

"How are you doing?" I said.

"I'm doing well. Better than I might have expected."

"I'm glad to hear that."

"I've actually given your friend a call. Your friend who works at St. Ann's. They said they might have an opening for a rookie teacher next year. Maybe you know all this already."

"No. I hadn't heard."

"I can't tell you how much I appreciate what you did for me.

You did exactly what I asked you to do. You gave me an understanding of why my husband died."

"I'm afraid I may have given you more of an understanding than you bargained for."

"It's true that I didn't expect to find out that he had hurt people. I didn't expect to find out that the person who killed him had reasons."

"He kept a lot of things concealed from you."

"Yes. He did. But it's strange…it still surprises me how quickly I was able to accept what Joanna Lipton was telling me. It was almost as if I'd always known that there was something missing from my picture of him. As if I'd always known there was a darker side."

Sometimes clients ask you to look into things and then hate you for what you find. It never bothers me much, and yet I was glad that Mrs. Carpenter hadn't ended up hating me for what I'd discovered about her husband.

"I'm sorry," she said, "that in order for you to find out what happened, two people had to die."

It had actually been four people, but I had seen no reason to tell her about Lee Macy or Amy Roth.

"And that you were the one who had to kill them. It must make you wish you'd never met me."

"I didn't have to kill them. I killed them because the person who employed them was intent on stopping the knowledge from coming out. It was his choice, and their choice. Not yours. Not mine."

"Is it hard to live with? Is it ever hard to sleep at night?"

Outside the window there was the sound of construction. The city was relentless.

I didn't see what either of us would gain from a discussion of my possibly troubled conscience.

"It's been an honor to work for you, Mrs. Carpenter. If you ever need any help again, I hope you'll remember me."

I got up from behind the desk. She stood up as well. I shook her hand.

"I'll remember you, all right," she said.

# Chapter thirty-four

Kate arrived for work a little later.

"I've been reading about you," she said. "How are you doing? There was an article that said you got shot in one of the tabloids."

"Don't believe everything you read," I said. "I was shot nowhere near the tabloids." A very old joke.

"Was that Mrs. Carpenter?"

"That was her."

"Not bad. Are you gonna date her?"

"Don't be vulgar, Kate. You don't date your clients."

"But she isn't your client anymore."

"You don't date your old clients either."

"Why not?"

"It's against the code."

"Oh, the code," she said. She put some water on for coffee. "I've been reading about the other one, too," she said. "Joanna Lipton."

Joanna had been in the front pages of all the newspapers for a few days. She'd even been written up in *People* magazine.

"What do you think is going to happen to her?" Kate said.

"It's hard to imagine any jury in the world coming down on her too harshly. Maybe she'll serve some time in a minimum security prison."

"I hope she doesn't. If I were in her shoes I would have wanted to run him over myself."

"Me too. But it'll probably be better for her soul if she serves some time for it."

"What about her father?"

"They've got a pretty good case against him. Conspiracy to commit murder, for starters. Whether he'll ever do any time, I have no idea. You can buy your way out of almost anything."

"I don't suppose the bastards from the drug company will ever have to pay for what they did."

My friend Addie Stone had written an investigative report that suggested that Weatherall knew that Carpenter was fixing the results of the drug studies to make the medication look safe and effective.

"Of course not. That's not how it works here in the land of the free."

"It's disillusioning."

"It *is* disillusioning," I said. "But we still have to do what we can."

# Chapter thirty-five

Later that day I took a drive to a cemetery near Tarrytown. In the main office I asked for directions to Amy Roth's grave.

It was near the top of a long hill. I walked up the hill slowly in the chilly, damp day.

There was a new fashion in gravestones. Maybe it had been around for a while, but I'd noticed it only recently. Many new gravestones had begun to bear photos of the deceased. On Amy Roth's stone, above her name and the dates of her birth and death, a laminated photograph was set in a recessed square. It was the picture I'd seen in her apartment: Amy and her niece on a visit to Disneyland.

In Jewish tradition, when you pay your respects to the dead, you leave a pebble on the gravestone to mark your visit. I didn't know how Amy Roth would feel about the gesture, but I found a small smooth rock and put it on top of her gravestone.

I went back to my car and drove into Tarrytown. I found a stationery store and bought writing paper and an envelope. Then I went to the diner where Amy had taken me, and I sat in the same booth that I'd sat in with her.

I took out the paper and a pen and wrote a letter to Amy's niece. It wasn't a long letter, because I didn't really know much about Amy. There was just one thing, really, that I wanted to tell her. I told her that her aunt Amy, as quiet and shy and nervous as she'd been, had also been as brave as anyone I'd ever known.

# About the Author

Raymond Miller is the *nom de plume* of a writer who lives in New York. This is his first Nathaniel Singer novel.

*The fonts used in this book are from the Garamond family*

28.74

**DATE DUE** *DAYS*

| AUG 2 0 2007 | | |
|---|---|---|
| AUG 2 6 2007 | | |
| SEP 0 2 2007 | | |
| NOV 1 1 2007 | | |
| DEC 1 3 2007 | | |
| JAN 0 3 2008 | | |
| FEB 1 2 2008 | | |
| MAY 1 8 2008 | | |
| JUN 1 4 2008 | | |
| WITHDRAWN | | |
| | | |
| | | |
| | | |
| | | |
| | | PRINTED IN U.S.A. |

GAYLORD